BLOOD OATH

THE EVERLASTING CHRONICLES

K.G. REUSS

EVERLY

"*P*lease," I sobbed, tugging against his hand. "Don't. Don't do this."

Raiden stopped his march and turned to me, his brows crinkling as he stared down at me beneath the twinkling stars just outside castle walls.

"I didn't do those things. I swear I didn't. It's not what you think. I was upset—"

He pressed his finger to my lips to silence me. A fat tear rolled down my cheek as he took me in. *General Raiden Hawthorne. Prince of Specials. My protector.* And now, my captor it seemed as he hauled my ass from Dementon grounds to Xanan, the capital city and center of the Special kingdom. I'd nearly killed him when Marcus and Nev's spell went awry. Hell, I'd nearly killed Nev when I'd found out it was a curse to keep me silent about being a Dyre member—a rebel group that was trying to overthrow the Xanan government and Order.

I sucked in sharp breath after sharp breath, my heart banging hard in my chest. I was the damn Mancer, a magical being—one of a kind—who could raise an army of the dead and take over. But here I was, having a damn panic attack as the man I loved hauled me in to be punished for attempted murder. Times two because I never screwed up a little. I always had to make it big.

"Breathe," he commanded.

It was the first word he'd spoken to me since he'd dragged me to the portal in the Conexus house basement.

I shook my head, dizzy from hyperventilating. I nearly dropped to my knees, but he caught me and held me tight to him before I felt the familiar crushing feeling of being shadow melded with him—one of his unique gifts that allowed him and members of Conexus to travel.

"Come," he said softly as we stopped our meld in the center of an empty courtyard.

Cobblestones and grass were underfoot. Two guards in dark armor with swords at their sides met us.

"General," one grunted as Raiden took my hand and led me through the gates to a large stone building.

"See to it that no one enters here," Raiden said to the guards.

"Yes, your highness," the second guard said.

It was so strange to hear him referred to that way, but I didn't have time to swoon over the fact my boyfriend was a prince or a general. Hell, if he was even still my boyfriend. I was certain attempted murder probably ended a relationship.

He led me into the stone building. It looked exactly how I'd figure a castle would look, only smaller. In the distance, I could make out the sounds of crying and moaning.

If I had to guess, these were the Xanan dungeons.

"You can enter the main castle through the doorway on the right," he said, leading me by my elbow. He nodded to guards at the door. "There are guards stationed at both sides of the door. No one escapes here."

That didn't bode well for me. Or Nev if they ended up bringing him here. Raiden had knocked him out with his sword during mine and Nev's fight. My heart went out to my vampire friend and the general of Dyre. I may have really screwed things up for the rebellion. And my family since they were part of the insurrection.

Of course, Raiden knew nothing of my involvement. Or at least I hoped he didn't, but judging by the fact I was being led into the dungeons, I'd say he might have an inkling.

We passed countless guards on our way to the dungeons. None of them stopped us, but why would they? Raiden Hawthorn was feared wherever he went. He'd even spent time in the dungeons himself trying to protect me, and for what? Just so he could toss me into a cell on my ass? It wasn't looking good for me. I just hoped he called my mom and made my death story sound unavoidable. And I hoped she didn't cry for long. When my end came, I didn't know who would execute me, but knowing Raiden led F.I.R.E. made me think it would be fitting for him to be my end. He was my beginning, after all.

The thoughts did nothing to calm me.

When we entered the dimly lit dungeons, I huddled against Raiden. The wails from the dark recesses made my skin crawl as I continued to gulp in mouthfuls of air.

Raiden conjured light in his hand and held it in his palm as he led us through the darkness to a cell deep within the dungeons.

"R-Raiden," I sniffled.

"Get in." The creak and clunk of the old cell opening was like a nail in my coffin.

I could probably fight him and maybe get away, but Raiden was Shadow, my protector. He was one of the strongest shifters and Specials in existence. I probably wouldn't get far.

To hell with it. I'd wanted to end all this shit a hundred times since I'd nearly died and Raiden had saved my life all those months ago on a highway in the middle of nowhere. Maybe this was fate saying it wasn't ready for my kind.

I'd try again in another life.

I stepped into the cell and closed my eyes as the door clanged close behind me. I heard it latch, and I choked down a whimper.

"This is for your own good, Everly," Raiden murmured before his footsteps faded in the darkness.

I wasn't mad. My resignation at the entire situation came fast. I was tired of fighting all the shit in my life. In that moment, lying down and admitting defeat seemed like a good idea, so I shuffled to a corner in the cell, curled up into a tight ball, and mourned my life. My mom. My friends. And Raiden.

Wails of pain and sadness echoed around me in the darkness. I knew there were prisoners nearby, but it was so dark I couldn't see them in their cells. In the distance, I heard strong clangs and then screams.

I curled tighter into myself and covered my ears.

If this was the end, it wasn't so bad. At least I wasn't being beaten deeper in the dungeon.

Yet.

RAIDEN

I stood guard outside the dungeons all night, my chest tight with worry. I didn't know what the hell I'd stumbled in on when I'd found Ever attacking Nev, but I knew it was nothing good. I could draw my conclusions.

And they sure as shit weren't singing the vampire's praises.

I'd needed to intervene before things went too far south. She'd been cursed. I knew that much. She'd attacked Nev. That was obvious. *But why?*

I'd nearly killed him when I saw him pinning her against the wall, but I gave him the benefit of the doubt and knocked him out instead. Now, he was sleeping it off under the watchful eye of the Conexus. I'd sent off a fire message to have Amanda, Sloane, and Jared spell a room in the house to hold the vampire in until I could get back and question him myself. Depending on what he told me, he'd end up free or he'd end up in the Xanan dungeons before he met my blade.

I couldn't shake the look of fear in Ever's eyes as I'd led her to her cell. I thought she'd beg and I'd give in, or that she'd try to fight me and run. But she'd stepped into the cage without looking back at me. That had me more worried than anything else at this point. That and her words, asking me if we were over.

Were we?

I did just throw her in prison, and she did try to murder me. I supposed I needed to figure out the reasoning behind it all before I made a decision about our future. She'd been about to tell me something important before she lunged for my knife and tried to gut me.

I breathed out. She'd been resigned to stepping into that dungeon. Like she was just giving up. I imagined her trying to breathe down there as she panicked. I knew she had to be going crazy.

I stepped forward to go back to her but stopped myself.

There's a reason you're doing this. You're protecting her. Saving her. She's strong. She'll be OK. She needs to learn that if she's slipped down a bad path, there are consequences. Hurt her now to save her later.

I swallowed and closed my eyes, my heart aching for her. I wasn't doing this to be cruel. Yes, I was pissed off, but this was about saving her before whatever she'd gotten herself into went too far. I'd let her out in the morning.

She'll be fine. She'll be OK. She's strong.

I repeated the words over and over as I watched the stars disappear from the night sky and give way to a serene blue.

The moment the sun hung in the morning sky, I rocketed back through the narrow corridors and went to her cell. It was so dark down there it was hard to see without light. I conjured some flames and moved to her cage. There, I found her curled into a tight ball on the floor in a corner.

Quickly, I unlocked the door and moved to her.

"Everly," I murmured, shaking her gently. "Wake up."

She didn't move.

I frowned and shook her again. "Ever. Come on."

She mumbled something I couldn't quite make out, so I lifted her into my arms and stood with her cradled to my chest. She curled into me as I carried her out of the dungeons and into the light of day. If the guards had anything to say to me, they certainly weren't brave enough as we passed by.

I took her back outside the gates of the castle and to the old tree that acted as a portal. I took the opportunity to look down at her to see her pretty face smudged with dirt and grime, her tears dried to her skin. Her body was cold, and I wanted to kick my own ass for not giving her my cloak to cover up with, but it was a cell, not a damn vacation. That was the whole point in it all. To show her what could happen if she kept up whatever she was doing.

I portaled us back to Conexus house and took her straight to her room by melding. Her eyelids fluttered open as she stared up at me before a look of soul crushing sadness crossed her face. I laid her in bed and swept her dark hair away from her face.

"We're home now. You should shower and rest. I'll have some food brought up for you."

She remained quiet, staring up at me with wavering eyes.

Eyes that said what she wasn't saying out loud.

She thought we were over. She'd asked as much, and I'd been vague and angry with her. *But how did one come back from leaving their soulmate in a damn cell all night?* I was an asshole and knew it, but I did it for her own good. It was my job to protect her. That didn't mean I had to pull punches because I loved her.

I pushed my healing into her, hoping it would help.

"We'll talk later." I backed away.

She used to reach for me and laugh whenever I'd back away. She'd tease me to come back. Tempting me with her green eyes and soft lips. Now, she only stared silently, no emotion on her face.

This may have been her breaking point.

But if keeping her safe meant she needed to be broken, so be it.

"Tell me everything." I leaned back in my leather chair behind my desk and stared at Nev.

Both his eyes were blackened, no doubt from his tussle with Everly the night before.

"Where is she? You took her. Tell me what you did to her," Nev snarled in his vorbex handcuffs as he sat in the chair in front of my desk, Eric and Damian on either side of him.

"She tried to kill you, so what do you care for?"

"She tried to kill you too," he snapped back. "Did you hurt her? I swear if you hurt her, you'll pay dearly."

I shifted forward in my seat and twined my fingers together as I stared at him.

"I sent her to the Xanan dungeons. Maybe she'll speak now and tell me what's going on without trying to kill me first. Of course, you know all about that curse, don't you, Blackburn?"

He sneered at me. "I don't know shit about shit."

"Everly didn't attack you for no reason. I want to know what's going on."

"She walked in on me fingering someone else. I assume that pissed her off a little considering everything."

I saw red.

I was on my feet and wrapping my hands around his throat in a matter of seconds.

"I will tear your fangs out of your head if you don't tell me what the hell I want to know." I squeezed his neck until his face turned red, then purple.

"Raiden." Damien stepped forward and rested his hands over mine, snapping me out of my rage.

I released Blackburn as he sucked in gulps of air, coughing and sputtering.

"You're insane," Blackburn wheezed out.

"She doesn't care about you. You know that," I said, going to stare out the window, not even sure if it was true.

Maybe he was right. Maybe she was pissed to find him with another girl. Maybe she still had feelings for him. Maybe the curse was just another attack on her to separate us.

"You took her to Xanan and left her in a dungeon. I say you'd be lucky if she gave a shit about you at this point," he rasped at me.

I swallowed and didn't bother to look back at him.

"You kill people through your interrogations. Why am I not in a Xanan dungeon being interrogated? Why am I your secret prisoner?" he continued. "If you're going to end me, then do it already."

"Get him out of here," I said softly. "He's free."

I heard the click of his vorbex cuffs unlatching and him rising from his seat.

He approached me, his boots thudding hard on the wooden floor.

"Don't hurt her," he said so only I could hear him. "She means everything to me. And to you. Keep her safe. The days are coming when she'll need you most. You know it's true. But know that when you fail her, I'll be there to pick up the pieces."

I turned and locked my gaze on him. His eyes were black as night in his lust. I swallowed down the painful gnawing in my throat and chest. It had been happening more frequently, and I didn't know what the hell it was. Ever since I'd bonded with Everly completely it had been there, growing stronger by the day.

Nev crinkled his brows at me, frowning. He rubbed his chest and shook his head like he could feel what I felt. That was ridiculous though. There was no way. He was a vampire. I was a shifter.

He turned on his heel and left, slamming the door behind him.

"Ever's awake," Eric said softly. "She's asking to see me."

I nodded tightly. Of course, she didn't want to see me first.

"Tell her I'd like to see her if she's OK with that."

"I'll tell her." He backed out of the room. leaving me with Damien.

"Shit's weird, Gen. Real weird." Damien let out a sigh and sank down in his seat. "First that damn curse we can't trace and then Blackburn. Then you leaving her in Xanan…"

"I wanted to show her what would happen if she kept on the path she's on."

"But man, you don't even know what path that is. You just threatened the life of Blackburn. He either didn't know shit or he's one hell of an actor. I think you made a mistake."

I sat back in my seat and let out a sigh.

"Something tells me there's more to it than that. I can feel it. I just… I don't know. I don't know what the hell it is. She said she joined something before the curse took hold. I know I probably messed up by reacting the way I did, but I really have her best interests at heart. I need to see her."

"She didn't join anything, man. That was probably the curse taking hold and making her say that shit. Another wedge to drive you apart. Let Eric talk to her. Maybe he can see where her head's at. Maybe he can get answers from her. The two of them are close."

I nodded and rubbed my eyes. "Yeah. OK."

"Relax. It could always be worse. She could tell you to go to hell and join the Cipher." I knew he meant it as a joke, but it was a serious matter.

Dead serious.

EVERLY

"Hey," Eric called out as he popped his head into my room. I'd summoned him through our Conexus mind connection earlier, knowing he was the first one I should talk to despite Raiden and my…. well, whatever the hell we were now.

"Hey." I swallowed and smoothed down my plaid Dementon skirt. "Come in."

Eric stepped into the room and came to my side. Neither of us said a word for a long time. I'd been over it a million times in my head how to start the conversation, but now it just wasn't coming to me, so I simply sat in awkward silence next to him.

"Sorry about the dungeons," he finally said.

I shrugged. "Sorry I tried to kill people."

He glanced at me, his lips quirking up into a smile. "Eh, what's new, right?" He bumped shoulders with me as I scoffed, shaking my head.

"I didn't mean it. I-I never wanted to hurt anyone, especially Raiden—"

"Ever, I know that. Raiden knows that too. We know you were cursed."

I nodded glumly. "Yeah. That sucked."

"Do you know who did it?" he asked carefully.

I let out a bitter laugh. "No."

I'd learned my lesson. I wasn't about to say shit this time. If Marcus and Nev were trying to teach me to keep my mouth shut, they knew how the hell to do it. My lips were sealed. I wondered how Eric's mind melding would work on me though if he decided to infiltrate my thoughts. Could he dig the truth from my head? The thought made my heart quicken. Eric always said he'd never done that to anyone unless he was forced to. Hopefully, he was never forced to with me.

Eric studied me for a moment. "OK. Well, how are you feeling?"

"Like shit," I muttered. "Nervous. Worried."

"Raiden isn't mad," he said gently.

"He seemed pretty pissed. He chucked my ass in the dungeons. I-I thought that was it, you know?" I bit my bottom lip, the ugly memory of the expression on his face through the shadows as he waited for me to step into the dark cell replaying in my mind.

"It wasn't. He just didn't know what the hell was going on, you know? Like, he didn't know if maybe you'd gotten into something you shouldn't have and needed to be reminded of your place." Eric sighed. "It's his place to explain himself to you. Not mine."

"It's OK. I'm sure you're not far off the mark."

"What are you going to do?"

I blew out a breath. "This life is dangerous. I knew it was. We're in the middle of this weird war where there are rats within the Order. The eradication of an entire breed of magical people is on the line. I'm... who I am." I picked at a piece of lint on my skirt. "I think I need to focus on being better. I got sidetracked. It won't happen again."

Eric frowned. "That sounds like you're going to make a decision you might regret."

I shrugged. "Maybe, but the way things are going, I won't be around long enough for it to matter. The Order, or someone in the Order, wants me dead. If I step foot outside Dementon grounds without one of you with me, my life becomes a game of survival. I mean, really, the decision is an easy one."

"Is it?" He surveyed me with his clear blue eyes.

"Unfortunately. I'm better off alone."

"Ever—"

"I need to focus. That's all. Maybe. . .someday. . ." my voice trailed off as acceptance washed over me.

Someday.

What a joke. I hated feeling sorry for myself, but there I was, really wallowing in it. The truth of the matter was, I did need to focus more. Maybe once I did, things would get better, and I'd survive the damn war and live my happily ever after. It was like my mom always said, *if it's meant to be, it'll be.* It won't have to be forced or fought for.

I had a long road ahead of me. May as well get on with it.

"Just. . . think it through. Don't make a decision in anger or desperation. Nothing is going to change. Shit will still be shit if you tell Raiden you're done because I know where that head of yours is."

"Psychic freak," I muttered, smiling a bit.

He winked at me. "You made me worse, you know."

"Sorry. Maybe we're almost even. You did bring me here, after all."

He laughed. "I saved your ass. We're even."

I smirked back, despite the feeling of despair. "I guess I should talk to Raiden."

"He's downstairs in his office. Nev just left." Eric studied me for a moment.

I was sure he was trying to check for my reaction.

I swallowed thickly. "Is Nev OK?"

"Yeah. Surly as always. Raiden released him. He had nothing to go on. Marcus was questioned as well. Nothing there, so for now, they're free to continue their shit."

"They're not bad guys."

"If you say so." He shook his head. "Come on. Let's get you fed and watered. You go talk to Raiden while I fix you something to eat. Sound good?"

"I guess," I mumbled, letting him pull me to my feet.

Wordlessly, we left my room and went downstairs. Thankfully, not many members seemed to be there. Damien was coming out of

Raiden's office, and Adam was breezing through the front door with Chloe. They both offered me smiles and waves before heading to the kitchen with Eric.

"Hey, Torres." Damien clapped me on the shoulder. "Missed you."

I stared at Raiden's closed door.

Damien glanced back at it before turning back to me. "It'll be fine. You're a brave girl. Go kick his ass."

"Right," I muttered as he moved past me to greet Adam and Chloe.

Hauling in a deep breath, I stepped to Raiden's door and knocked gently. I could've just spoken through our connection, but that felt awkward given the circumstances.

The door opened a moment later as Raiden sat at his desk. He must have used his powers to do it because he was rifling through papers and didn't even look up.

I cleared my throat, drawing his attention from the disarray on his desk.

Immediately, he was on his feet and moving toward me. Everything about his movement suggested how powerful he was—how powerful he could be.

"Everly," he said in that deep rumble of his.

I closed the door and stepped deeper into his office, rubbing my arms for comfort. He was less than a foot away from me as he stared down at me with his aquamarine eyes, keen and filled with what I assumed was worry.

"Are you well?" he asked softly, his gaze sweeping over me. "I can have some food brought in—"

"Eric is making me something," I said, rubbing my arms again.

"Are you cold? I can get you a blanket—"

"I think we should break up," I blurted out at the same time he spoke and reached for a blanket hanging over the edge of a chair near the door.

"What?" he demanded, everything about him switching gears from his facial expression to the way his hands curled into fists.

"I think we should break up."

His Adam's apple bobbed in his throat for a moment before he spoke, "I'm sorry for what I did to you. I only wanted to make sure you knew what would happen if you were involved in something—"

I held my hand up to stop him. "I know. And it's OK. Really. I probably deserved it. I mean, I did try to kill you. And Nev. And myself. And would've probably hurt someone else if they'd gotten in my way. So, yeah. I get it. I would've locked me up too."

"Everly—"

"You don't need to explain yourself, Shadow. Your job is to protect, and that's what you were doing. I understand," I said, pulling the engagement ring off my finger and holding it out to him in my palm. "My job is to stay safe and a million other things. I lost focus. I fell so hard for you. I think it was probably the best and worst idea I've ever had."

He watched me wordlessly as I licked my lips.

"I want us to both be free. I'm dangerous." My last sentence came out in a choked whisper as my hand shook, wobbling the ruby and diamond ring.

"You're not, baby," he said softly, reaching out and closing his hand around mine until I clutched the ring in our hold.

His hand trailed from mine, and he gathered me to his body in a fierce hug. As much as I wanted to pull away and run from the reality of my life, I let him hold me. His fingers raked through my hair as he tightened his hold on me.

"Do you feel this?" he asked softly. "The way I hold you? How perfectly you fit in my arms? The way our hearts beat as one? You are mine, Everly. I'm not letting you go. I love you with everything I am. I overreacted. I was so sick with worry. It was the best idea I had. I trust you. I trust *in* you. I know you had nothing to do with any of that shit. You wouldn't. *You just wouldn't.*" He kissed the top of my head fiercely, making me feel even worse because he was wrong—I was the center of that shit storm.

"I'm not letting you go. I'm not letting you leave me. You're going to be my queen. My wife. You are *everything* to me. I love you so much it's tearing me apart inside. I can't lose you. We can't lose one another. Trust me, OK? Please, believe that. This isn't about being pissed off with one another. It's about knowing we are one, and we're stronger together than apart. That you love me like I love you. We both made mistakes. I'm sorry for mine."

I twisted my fingers into his black uniform shirt. "What if it gets worse?"

"Then it gets worse, and we overcome it. We're a team. You and me. Look at me." He tilted my chin up and brushed a tear away from my cheek. "I'd die for you. I'm with you always. No matter the path. I swear it."

"I love you," I said in a shaky voice. "I don't want you to be hurt—"

"I won't be. My job is to protect you, the love of my life. And I'll never leave your side. Nothing will stop me from being there for you. Believe me, Everly."

The way he looked down at me made my guts clench. I knew his words were true. He'd be there until the bitter end, should it come down to that. Truth be told, I loved him so much I wasn't sure I could manage not being with him. I didn't know if it was our soul bond or just love, but I felt it all the way to my core. But I'd leave to keep him safe. I knew that without having to think about it. If it came down to it, I'd go. To save him, I'd leave.

That was my out. Run. Selfishly, I could maintain what we had by telling I myself I could always run if I had to.

"Stay with me," he murmured, leaning down, his lips close to mine. Without breaking away, he took the ring from my hand and pushed it back onto my finger.

"I'll stay."

His lips collided against mine, and it was like every worry and thought flew out of my head as he held me. Everything about Raiden, my Shadow, felt right.

Even if everything else felt so damn wrong.

EVERLY

"*L*eft. Right. Duck, baby. Yes. Just like that." Raiden's sword whipped around me. "Block. Kick."

A whoosh of air left him as I planted my foot in the center of his chest and sent him stumbling backward. Seeing an opening, I rushed forward and swept my foot out, knocking him to the ground. He tumbled down. I wasted no time hopping on him and straddling him.

I crushed my lips to his in a deep kiss. His hands tightened on my waist as he held me before they traveled to my ass where he gripped my cheeks.

"I win," I breathed out against his lips as his hard length pressed against my heat. I shifted against him, making him groan into my mouth as I kissed him again.

We were supposed to be practicing. He'd wanted me to get better with the sword. He'd decided instructing me in each move would be the best way to get me comfortable with the weapon.

"I gladly accept the loss," he said, nipping at my bottom lip.

It had been nearly two weeks since everything went down with Nev. I hadn't seen him on campus but hadn't made it a point to look for him. He wasn't in my dreams either. I assumed he was pissed at me over trying to spill about our secret rebel group to Raiden.

A shriek left my lips as Raiden flipped me onto my back, his erection pressed firmly between my legs as he surveyed me from above. He twined his fingers through mine and brought them over my head as he kissed me. I slid my tongue against his, relishing in his heat.

"Now that's what I call a practice," Damien's voice boomed out in the gym.

Raiden groaned against my lips before pulling away from me and fixing Damien with a stern look.

"It's motivation," Raiden said easily, not moving off me. He winked down at me as I let out a laugh.

"Nice. Hey, Sloane," Damien shouted as the door banged closed. "Shadow says this is how he motivates Ever. Think I can motivate you the same way?"

"You don't have anything I want to be motivated with, Wick," she called out.

Raiden chuckled as Damien let out a loud laugh. I watched as Raiden's aquamarine eyes took in Damien and Sloane.

I shifted beneath him, the awkwardness of him not moving and displaying our *technique* to Conexus making my face heat with embarrassment. As if sensing my discomfort, he shifted off me and hauled me to my feet. He pecked my lips before focusing back on Damien and Sloane.

"Gen, did you get something to wear to the Arcane Ball? It's coming up soon," Sloane said, sitting down to stretch.

Raiden glanced to me before answering, "Uh, I'm sure I have something in my closet. I go to enough of these events I should have something I can use."

"Same. I'll just wear my suit from last year," Damien said as he sat to stretch across from Sloane.

"Ever, do you have something to wear?" Sloane came out of a long stretch and fixed her gaze on me.

"Uh, I-I don't think I'll be going—"

Raiden swung his focus to me. "Of course, you're going. All of

Conexus goes. I, uh, actually need to talk to you about it anyway."

Sloane glanced between us but didn't say anything as she leaned into another stretch.

"Raiden, I can't afford a fancy dress," I started, my voice soft, but he pressed his fingers to my lips to quiet me.

"My queen will want for nothing. I'll take care of it," he murmured, lifting my hand and pressing his lips to the ring only he and I could see.

Butterflies took flight in my stomach as he let his fingers drift away and turned his attention to Damien.

"Did you tell Adam that I need him to do my patrol tonight until I get back?"

"Yep." Damien got to his feet and stretched his arms. "He was cool with it."

"Where are you going?" I asked.

"That's what I need to talk to you about." He offered me a quick smile. "We're done with practice if you have a moment."

"Gosh, I don't know. I have a meeting at two with a suspicious rotwraith, and then I need to wash my hair at three—"

He smirked at me and tugged my hand to lead me out of the gym. "Come on."

"Don't do anything I wouldn't do," Damien called out as Sloane waved at us.

Raiden let out a soft laugh and held the door for me. I stepped outside into the sunshine. We didn't typically spend a lot of time out in the light, but I happened to enjoy a calm afternoon when the snow was glistening.

"It's cold," Raiden said, wrapping his arm around my waist and flicking his wrist. Warmth surrounded us, and I knew he was using one of his magic spells to keep us from freezing.

"Thanks." I snuggled closer to him as we strolled back to the Conexus house.

We didn't pass a single student the whole way there. Not that it mattered. They tended to scamper away like roaches in the light whenever Conexus members were close.

19

"What did you want to talk about?" I asked as the snow crunched beneath our boots.

He was quiet for a moment before he spoke, "I know I said we could wait to share our engagement, but I think we should announce it."

I stopped. "You said you'd give me time—"

"And I didn't lie." He halted and stared down at me. He brushed a piece of my dark hair away from my face. "We *will* wait. It's just I think we should at least announce it at the ball. Everyone will be there. I think it's important I make my intentions clear. People are looking at me to be their new king. I need to show how serious I am about it."

I winced. I understood where he was coming from. That didn't mean I liked the idea more though.

"And you swear we can still wait on a wedding?"

"Absolutely. I swore I wouldn't push you about a date for it. I won't. We can even sweep off the midnight before I take the throne and do it. We'll be cutting it close, but I don't care. I just want you any way I can have you."

That was twice in an hour he made butterflies take flight in my body.

"OK," I said, leaning in to kiss him. "We can announce it."

He hauled me closer. "You're so perfect. Thank you, Ever."

"For what?"

"For everything. You make me so unbelievably happy. I never knew love could be like this."

I wrapped my arms around his neck and kissed him again. The familiar tug of his shadow melding washed over us. When it stopped, I broke the kiss off to see where he'd taken us.

"We worked up a sweat," he said with a smile as the water in his shower turned on with his magic.

"Why do I feel like we're going to work up another?" I lifted a brow at him.

"Because my girl is psychic."

I giggled as he made fast work of removing our clothes and

leading me into the shower. The moment we were beneath the spray, he pinned me against the wall, his fingers tangled in my hair as he hoisted me up so my legs wound around his waist.

"I want you," he rasped between fevered kisses.

"You have me," I breathed against his lips as he moved his hand to cradle my breast. I let out gasp as he thrust up into me, filling me completely.

My head fell back against the wall. The warm water pelted us as he worked his magic on me, his lips at my neck. My body jostled against the wet tiles with every fevered thrust of his body into mine.

"Raiden," I whimpered as he buried himself deep inside me over and over. A sweeping heat took hold as he coaxed my release to the surface. His lips met mine again when my walls clenched around his thickness.

He let out a string of curses and tumbled through the euphoria with me, both of us clinging to one another.

Breathless, his movements slowed, and he rested his forehead against mine.

"I've never loved anyone like I love you," he murmured. "It scares me."

I cradled his face and made him look at me. "Why?"

"Because of what I'd do if I ever lost you." His Adam's apple bobbed as he studied me. "My goodness would turn black. I know I'd tear this world apart in my heartache and anger."

My heart skipped at his admittance.

"I wouldn't want that," I said gently. "I'd want you to be happy."

"I would *never* be happy without you, Everly." His lips brushed mine. "You are my happiness. I love you."

"I love you too," I whispered back, my heart in my throat.

All sorts of terrifying thoughts swirled through my mind. Me and Dyre. Having to leave. Hoping it never came to that. Praying I could get Raiden on our side so we wouldn't have to be without each other.

And knowing I had to talk to Nevron Blackburn.

Sooner rather than later.

RAIDEN

After the best shower of my life, we got out, and I toweled Ever off. I tossed the cloth aside and stalked toward her, unable to resist her naked beauty. My cock hardened at the thought of being inside her again.

"More?" she asked with a laugh, backing away from me.

"Always." I pounced, tossing her gently onto my mattress.

I pushed myself back inside her tight heat, leisurely thrusting to fan the flames of desire that were rarely banked between us.

She was always so wet and ready for me. It drove me mad as I thrust inside her.

"Mm, baby," I groaned softly as goosebumps erupted along my skin at how good she felt wrapped around my dick. "What you do to me."

She dragged her fingernails through my silver hair, making me let out a feral growl against her soft lips.

"Spread your legs wider," I rasped. "I want to be deeper."

She did as asked, opening up more for me. Her green eyes locked on mine as I snapped my hips forward, shoving deeper into her small, tight body.

"Fuck," I choked out. "God, you feel so good, baby."

She let out the sexiest little gasp as I drilled into her heat, her nails in my back as she clung to me.

Within moments, she was trembling beneath me and crying out against my lips. Her body shook with her release, teasing me with mine. Unable to hold off, I spilled myself inside her amid a low groan, the pleasure rushing through my body.

I could stay this way forever. . .

I let out a shaky breath as I rested my forehead against hers.

"You're amazing, Everly," I murmured.

Her long eyelashes fluttered and a tiny smile graced her plump lips. "You're pretty amazing too."

I smiled at that and placed a kiss on her lips before slipping from her heat. I dragged her against my body, relishing in her warmth.

"Nap time," she murmured, snuggling against my chest. In moments, her breathing grew deep, letting me know she'd fallen asleep.

I held her for as long as I could before I eased off the bed and draped my blankets over her body. The last thing I wanted to do was leave her, but I had a meeting I needed to get to.

Quietly, I got dressed, my throat tight. I'd been so afraid when she'd come in to tell me she wanted to break up. There was no way. Just no way I'd let her go. I'd never loved or cared for anything as much as I did for her in my entire life. I only wanted to make things work. I wasn't exactly great at relationships, but damn it, I was trying.

"I'll be back soon," I whispered, kissing the top of her head gently. "I love you."

A tiny smile cut her lips up as she snuggled deeper into bed. I watched her for another minute before I forced myself to meld into the shadows and head to Xanan.

NIGHT HAD FALLEN, and I sat staring at my father.

"I assume you have something important to talk to me about," Father said with a grunt as he settled in his chair behind his desk.

24

Everything was always so official with him. He didn't even feel like a father to me anymore. Everything that had made him my father left when my mother had been found murdered when I was twelve. Now it was just the proper bullshit that came with dealing with royalty.

"Yes." I exhaled. "I'm engaged to be married."

He stilled, not saying a word.

"We haven't set a date, but it won't be anytime soon. I thought it would be best to announce it at the Arcane Ball and make it official."

He locked eyes with me. "To the mancer?"

I bristled. "Yes, to Everly Torres."

"You do realize your union could end the world, right?" A muscle thrummed along his jaw.

"I'm aware of the potential, but I've taken the Vow of Eternity. I belong to her. *Forever.*" I needed to make that clear to him.

"You belong to the girl until her death—"

"Which I can bring her back from," I interrupted, my patience growing thin.

It was no secret Father didn't want me with her. He'd done everything in his power to keep me away from Ever, including arranging a marriage to Amara.

I bristled, anticipating a fight from him. It wouldn't matter what he said or did. I wasn't going to back down on this. I'd taken the vow. There wasn't shit anyone could do about it now.

He sighed and was quiet for a moment before he spoke, "Raiden, you may think me cruel and a fool. I'm neither of those things. I want your happiness. Truly. You're a lot like your mother. She always wanted to save the world too. You know where that got her? Sealed in a tomb in the family crypt."

I ground my teeth as I listened to him. "I wasn't asking for your permission or your opinion—"

"But you're damn well going to get it," he snapped at me. "This isn't a game, boy. Your fiancée could perish because of your arrogance. You could lose her like I lost your mother!" He pounded his fist on the mahogany desk and stared me down.

I didn't answer him, allowing him the time he needed to cool down. His words hit me hard though.

Not once in all the years since my mother's passing had he shown any sign he missed her. He'd grown rigid and cold, but he'd never acknowledged her loss like he was now. It gave me pause, curious about what he'd say next.

"Your mother wasn't the woman you thought she was," he said softly, settling back in his seat and rubbing his eyes.

"What?" I frowned at his words.

"Your mother. Helena." He let out a soft chuckle. "What a beauty. Adventurous. Stubborn. Beautiful. *Secretive.*"

He rose to his feet and went to his bar to pour two glasses of tarish. I watched in confusion, wondering what the hell he was talking about. He returned a moment later with the bottle and two glasses. He slid my glass to me.

"Our marriage was arranged. Helena didn't love me in the beginning. I don't even know if she ever did, but I thought myself the luckiest bastard in all the world to have been blessed with such a beautiful wife. The fae are always beautiful." He swirled the liquid in his glass as I sipped mine.

The last thing I wanted to do was interrupt if he was going to open up to me, so I sat in silence, waiting.

"I heard the rumors." He took a deep swallow and placed his glass down, growing silent once more.

"What rumors?" I sat forward. I'd never heard rumors about my mother. Not before her death. Certainly not after.

"Of her being in love with another man and being forced to leave him to marry me. That I was the reason for her sadness. She cried every night the first year we were married." He grew somber, his voice shaking.

My heart clenched at his words. I hadn't known that.

"Mother did love you though," I said softly.

"In her own way, perhaps," he said with a nod. "I loved her with my entire being. She loved me with her mind, never her heart. Or at least not all of it. I'd always be the man who took her from the one she truly loved."

"Who was he?" I dared ask.

He scoffed and shook his head before finishing his drink and pouring another glass. He was quiet for so long that I didn't think he was going to answer me.

Finally, he spoke.

"Aviram," he said thickly.

My heart plummeted at his words.

"Aviram. . . the vampire overlord?" I wasn't sure if I'd heard him correctly.

"Rumor has it." Father refilled our glasses again.

"Why are you telling me this?"

He shrugged. "I figured you should know. It's not the end of the story though. I got her pregnant after two years of marriage. With you and a sibling."

I leaned forward further, my breath catching. "What?"

He nodded. "You were a twin, my son. She went into labor and delivered two boys. You survived. Your brother didn't. I didn't even see his body. I focused on what I had, instead of what I'd lost. Perhaps that was where I went wrong. I'd only just gotten Helena to care about me when we lost your twin. She withdrew from me again. But I had you. A healthy son. An heir to my throne. Beautiful like your mother. Strong. Smart. And beyond *special*."

I had no idea I'd had a brother. A twin. The news floored me.

"What was his name? My brother?" I asked softly, my heart aching for a sibling I'd never had the chance to know.

Father drank again before answering. "Kazimir Wesley Hawthorne."

Kazimir. Kaz. My brother. I was a twin. My mother's words at Brighton's office telling me to find my brother. But how could I find him if he was dead?

"Why have I never seen his tomb in the crypts?"

"Your mother begged for him to be buried in the place she grew up, Ravenvale Grove, a Special village just outside London. I agreed because I didn't want anyone to know I'd lost a son. I didn't want my genes to look weak." He let out a soft huff of sad laughter before continuing, "He was taken and laid to rest in her family's crypt. She traveled with you and the body of your brother there. I stayed behind to deal with Order business. And here we are."

"Why was I never told?" I asked as he refilled my glass once more. "And why now?"

"Because it didn't matter then. He was gone. You were here. As for why now, I think it should be obvious, Raiden." He nodded for me to drink, so I did.

"Why?" I pressed as he refilled my glass once more.

"Because you're all I have left, and your life is in danger. There are snakes within the Order. There are those who wish to take our power, our throne, from us. They're plotting, waiting for us to expose our weaknesses before they strike. They'll stop at nothing to do it. How do you even know you're in love, Raiden? A pretty face and a few nights between a girl's legs doesn't equate to love. Marrying the mancer is a grave mistake."

"It's not a mistake, Father," I said, finishing my drink. "And even if it were, it's mine to make."

"I don't want you harmed. Our kingdom would fall. And not just if you marry her. If you *lose* her. If you love her the way you claim to, losing her would mean losing you. Trust me when I say losing those we love can change your entire world." He leaned back in his seat, breathing hard.

"Father, I took the Vow of Eternity for her. If I decided to not go through with my marriage to her, there isn't any way for me to produce an heir unless she dies. It brings us full circle because I love her with *every* ounce of my being and a world without her in it is a world I don't want to live in."

He visibly swallowed as he surveyed me. When he finally spoke, his voice was gruff, "Drink up. Maybe with your mind loose, you'll realize what I'm saying to you."

I slammed back my drink as he poured me another. "And what is that?"

"That *she* is your weakness. If you marry her, you run the risk of

28

her powers overwhelming us. You two have already gotten too close. If she is killed, your heartbreak could end us all. Her death could be your undoing. Do you not see that?"

"That's the thing, Father. I would never let her die. It is my job as her reever to ensure her survival."

"Your duty is to your people. To the throne! Don't throw it away, Raiden. She will be used against us. Listen to me, she's in danger just as much as you are—"

I finished my drink and got to my feet. "We're done here. I'll make my announcement at the Arcane Ball. I *will* marry Everly, and I will take out anyone who dares harm her. To hell with anyone who tries to use us. We're the ones in control. *We* decide our paths. Not some damn prophecy or corrupt old men."

I didn't wait for him to answer me. I swept from his office and portaled out of there.

It wouldn't matter anyway. I knew where he stood on the subject and I knew where I stood.

Nothing was ever going to change that.

EVERLY

I wandered across the Dementon grounds alone. It was well after two in the morning, and I was supposed to be doing my patrols. And I was. Chloe had turned up and started walking with me and Adam. I'd decided to give them some time alone. Adam protested weakly, but after I'd sworn I wouldn't't tell anyone, he'd happily run off with Chloe, promising they owed me one. I knew they hadn't been able to see each other as often lately because of differing schedules and Raiden sending them off on separate missions. This was my small gift to them.

Dementon was probably the safest place in the world for me. Alone, outside its gates, I didn't stand much of a chance. That was why I felt relatively OK as I strolled through the darkened grounds in the dead of night.

The sound of a stick snapping in the nearby forest made me freeze for a moment. I peered through the darkness, my vision heightened from the gifts I'd gotten from the other members of Conexus. When I saw nothing, I kept moving.

Moments later, the sound of footsteps behind me made me whip around to find nothing but low hanging fog. Breathing out, I turned back only to come face-to-face with a hungry vampire.

I let out a scream right before a warm hand came from behind me and covered my mouth. My pulse roared in my ears as I struggled against my captor.

"Shh," Marcus murmured in my ear. "It's us." His hand dropped from my face as I relaxed.

"What the hell are you guys doing?" I hissed, swiveling my glare between them.

"Looking for you," Nev said, quirking a brow at me.

"Well, you found me." I glanced around to make sure no one was around us.

Marcus must have understood my worries because he flicked his wrist. Instantly, a thin shimmer covered us, so we were hidden from anyone nearby.

"We need to talk," Nev continued, his typical upbeat self not present. In its place was someone gruff. And hungry if I were being honest. His eyes had taken on the color of the night with his hunger. He always seemed cranky when he was near a bloodlust.

"Follow us," Marcus said before I could answer.

Knowing we really did need to talk, I fell in step next to them. No one spoke the entire way to the Place, the secret meeting spot on campus for Dyre. Once inside, I took a seat on an overstuffed couch and waited for someone to break the silence.

"You almost burned down my place. You tried to kill me," Nev said, crossing his arms and leaning against the wall across from me.

"You and Marcus almost killed me *and* you choked me," I shot back. "Did you know I fell on Raiden's knife and it went through my guts? If he hadn't been there with the guys, I would've bled out."

"That's the price for silence," Nev said with a grunt, looking away from me. A muscle feathered along his jaw.

"You're being an ass." I turned to Marcus who settled into the chair beside the sofa I was on. "Are you going to be an ass too?"

"You knew the rules, Ever. We're just really disappointed." Marcus let out a sigh and shook his head.

"You assholes cast a spell on me that could have killed me." I glared from one of them to the other. "That's messed up, even for you."

"What's messed up is you not telling us and letting us help," Nev said. "You don't run the show, Ever. I do. I'm your general here—"

"You're *a* general, yes, but ultimately, I'm in charge. *I* choose."

He let out a sigh and stared upward like it was going to help him get his thoughts together.

"You do understand why we're worried, right?" Marcus asked. "You're supposed to be helping us, yet you were trying to spill secrets."

"It wasn't like I set out to blab about it to anyone who'd listen. I was telling Shadow—"

"Oh, just say his name," Nev snapped. "No sense in beating around the bush about it. You know who he is. *I* know who he is. Stop trying to hide it."

I stared at the hungry vampire before me, frozen. "Y-you know who Shadow is?"

"Of course, I know. I mean, I didn't at first, but I had my suspicions. You said you were telling Shadow. Then I hear you attacked Raiden. It didn't take a genius to work that one out." A muscle thrummed along his jaw again. "So just say it. Say Hawthorne is Shadow so we can move on to the next part."

"What's the next part?" I swallowed as I waited for an answer.

Nev moved forward until he was kneeling in front of me. "We get him on our side or we kill him."

"You can't kill him," I snarled. "He's my Reever—"

"And if he takes control of you and our currently really bad situation, he owns you. If you align with him, we're screwed. My *entire race* is on the line. *My* people could perish because of it." Nev pounded his chest, his near-black eyes blazing. "I can't allow that to happen."

"He won't do that. He promised he'd go where I went—"

"If it serves his needs, Ever. Wake up."

"I am awake!" I made to push him away, but he lunged forward and pinned me to the couch.

"Let me go!" I shoved at him, but he held fast.

"Why can't you see reason?" he demanded. "Why? What will it take? Hawthorne is our enemy until he proves otherwise. You're getting too close to him—"

"I love him!" I shouted, done with fighting Nev. "*I love him*. He asked me to marry him, and I said yes."

Nev let out a snarl, pushed off me, and twisted his fingers in his blond hair.

"Is the ring glamoured?" Marcus asked softly.

I wiped at my eyes and nodded as he reached forward to take my hand.

"It's a good spell. Probably better than one I could do," he said, surveying it. "I can barely see the trace magic on it. I wouldn't have even been able to tell if you hadn't confirmed it for me." He waved his hand over mine, and the thin veil of magic slipped away, revealing my ring to him.

He stared down at it for a moment, a frown on his face. "Nev? Look at this."

Nev closed his eyes for a moment before stomping forward and glaring down at the black diamonds and ruby.

"A vampire ring?" Nev scoffed, some emotion flitting over his face I couldn't quite place. "What's he playing at?"

"His mother loved rubies," I said, yanking my hand away. "She asked for them in her crown but his father refused. It's a way to honor her."

"They say the queen was a good soul," Marcus murmured. "I have no doubt if she were still alive, none of this would be happening to us all right now."

"She was fae," I whispered. "A psy like me. Like Raiden."

"Hawthorne is a shifter," Nev said, frowning.

"He's more than that. It's true, he's a shifter, but he's also capable of weaving spells and has psy abilities. He has the ability to possess all abilities," I said softly.

"Except vampirism." Nev licked his lips and looked back at my ring. "Regardless of his mother's love for rubies, it doesn't make sense to me why he'd want his queen to wear them."

"I told you why." I sighed, not in the mood for the argument. "His mother—"

"No, Nev has a point," Marcus said, nodding. "If Hawthorne

announces you as his bride, *our* world will see the ring. This ring, Ever, is a *big* deal."

"I get that rubies are for vampires—"

"Just show her." Marcus glanced at Nev. "Then maybe she'll understand."

"Show me?" I crinkled my brows as Nev pulled his wallet out of his pocket.

He thrust a photo at me of two hands—a man's and a woman's. A wedding photo showcasing their rings over a bouquet of wildflowers.

"What is this?" I stared at the ring she was wearing.

It looked hauntingly similar to mine, right down to the black band and cut stones.

"That's my mother's ring. Aviram's queen, Lena. Her ring has a striking resemblance to yours. He had it custom made for her. He buried her with it."

"It's probably just a coincidence," I murmured, not sure what to even make of it.

It had to be a coincidence. *How would Raiden know the bride of the vampire overlord had damn near the same ring as his mother?*

Marcus waved his hand over mine, the thin veil of magic sliding back in place to shield my ring again.

"It's. . . something." Nev sighed and flopped down beside me, jostling me.

We were all quiet for a moment before I spoke, "I want to save people. I'm still in Dyre if you'll have me. I'll try to get Raiden in with us."

"I think that's acceptable. You can't tell him about us, so it's going to be hard. And since the damn Conexus general is now the guy we need, it's really going to be hard. Raiden is still on the side of the Order. He's still their yes man. It's going to be hard to convert that, no matter what you say or do. Do you understand that it may come down to something not so good?" Marcus asked quietly.

I swallowed thickly. "I'm aware, but I *know* Raiden. He'll follow me. He promised he would."

"You can't tell him straight out. We need to drop breadcrumbs so he can see for himself. Despite his promise to follow blindly, Hawthorne isn't a fool. He'll require proof. And if we just announce ourselves to him, he'll haul our asses to Xanan for interrogation. We can't risk it." Nev rested his head against the back of the couch and closed his eyes. "This is a nightmare. I really hoped it was Craft or even Wick. I think they would've been easier to convert."

"They said they'd follow me too," I murmured.

"And they're just like Hawthorne," Nev grunted. "No one is dumb enough to blindly follow. Chaos is imminent, I'm afraid." Nev grew quiet. "Ever?"

"Yeah?"

"Would you leave *him*? Hawthorne. Break ties with him and run if you had to?"

Would I? We were a pair. A couple. Soul bound. *Could I walk away and just be done in order to save the world?*

"Yes," I said, my voice thick with emotion. I didn't want it to come to that, but I would if it did. "I would. But it's not going to come to that. I really believe he'd follow me if I had to go. Can you give me time to figure out a plan?"

"What choice do we have? We can't just murder the damn prince and Reever. What a mess," Nev mumbled, rubbing his eyes.

I studied his pale form, deciding we needed a change of subject. He looked like he was wasting away. The color was gone from his skin, and he had a waxy, dead look about him. His eyes were darkening by the minute as he fought his bloodlust.

"When was the last time you fed?" I crinkled my brows as I stared at him.

"I don't know. Few days," he muttered.

"Drink from me," I whispered, breathing out.

I hated offering. It felt like a betrayal to Raiden, but I wanted Nev to trust me again. I couldn't have him contemplating killing Raiden. Offering myself as a meal seemed like the best option. Show him I trusted him and maybe he'd trust me in return sort of thing.

He cracked an eyelid open and cocked his head as he peered at me. "You're offering yourself to me?"

"Yes, but just a drink. Nothing sexual. You're a moody prick when you're thirsty."

A tiny smile cut his lips up. "I blame my fluctuating blood sugar." He paused and studied me. "Can I bite you anywhere?"

"Do you promise to heal it?" I countered.

"Absolutely," he said, his voice soft and silky.

It sent a flurry of goosebumps along my skin. He was already turning on that vampire seduction. Raiden's face flashed in my mind, making me hesitate. But earning Nev's trust back was the best way for me to ensure Raiden's safety.

"Then yes," I said reluctantly. Wincing, I pulled away.

"Marcus, leave us," Nev murmured, his gaze fixed on me.

"Be careful to not drain her too much." Marcus got to his feet and backed away. "I'll wait outside."

When he left I peeked at Nev.

"Come here." He patted his lap.

"Nev—"

"You *said* I could do it anywhere. And as much as I'd like to get between your legs to do it, I'm trying to be a gentleman about this, so please, Everly dear, come sit on my lap so I can feed. Respectfully."

My face heated at his words, and I shot him a glare. He smirked back at me and patted his thighs again. Sighing, I slid over until I was on his lap and looking at him.

"Close your eyes," he said softly.

I shut my eyes, my heart pounding hard. His fingers grazed along my cheek before they moved lower to my neck.

"You're so scared. Don't you trust me?" His lips brushed against my cheek.

"I trust you," I whispered thickly as his hand moved to rest over my heart.

It didn't stop the worry though. I knew how powerful his bite could be. I knew giving willingly to a vampire, especially, Nevron Blackburn, was an intimate affair.

"Your heart is thundering so hard. It has been since the moment I *caught* you. Why are you so afraid?"

His soft voice and touch were doing something to me. My head felt cloudy as he cradled me against his chest. Being alone with Nev was always dangerous business.

"Because I don't know why I feel this way whenever we're close," I admitted.

He let out a soft chuckle. "I have a few theories, my dear."

I gasped as he licked along my collarbone before his warm lips pressed a kiss to it. I tried to keep Raiden at the forefront of my mind as my anchor, but Nev was determined to push those thoughts away with his sultry tone and touch.

"Do you remember our night together?" he murmured against my skin.

"Yes," I rasped, struggling internally with aligning my thoughts so I could regain control of my body.

"Do you remember when I touched you?"

I nodded wordlessly as he skimmed his knuckles along the tops of my breasts. Before I could push his hands away, he sank his teeth into my neck, causing a moan to work its way from my lips. All sorts of delicious feelings flooded my body. He tightened his hold on me as he drank.

He withdrew his fangs just as quickly as he'd sunk them into me and licked along the hurt he created. If I thought my head was cloudy before, it was nothing compared to what it felt like now. If he commanded me to drop to my knees for him, I knew I would. I wouldn't have a choice. But this was the ultimate show of trust. Everything about the lust he left behind from his voice to his bite screamed control. It was why I was so scared to let him bite me again. I knew the reaction my body had to his fangs and the guilt that would follow.

"Do you remember touching me? Rubbing me?" he asked as his lips skimmed along my collarbone again. "Do you remember how hard I came?"

Frowning, I shook my head in confusion. I swallowed, trying desperately to regain control of my mind and body. This was why it was so hard to put my trust into him. He always took things too far.

"Answer me," he commanded, pulling at some invisible cord deep in my soul.

"Yes," I choked out.

A fuzzy memory of him calling out my name as his body shook flashed in my mind.

"Do you remember when you came for me? Do you remember all the things we did to each other that night? How wet you were for me? How hard I was for you?"

Truth of the matter was I didn't, but I was too foggy headed to question him. Instead, I clung to the memory that was near the surface. The one where we'd kissed and touched, and he'd torn the buttons from my shirt before guiding my hands to his zipper. Everything got hazy in my head after that. Things had ended there. We'd woken up with our clothes on when Damien and Brandon had burst into Nev's dorm.

Right?

"Did you know one of my powers is mind control? I can befuddle your mind and make you think things. Make you do things. Make you *forget* things. I can make you a little puppet on my string."

I whimpered as the fogginess grew heavier. His hand trailed lower until it was resting on my abdomen.

"Now, ask me your question." He ran his nose along my jaw. "Because I know my sweet mancer has one."

"Did we ...did we have sex?" *That couldn't be right.* We hadn't. I'd have known. *What the hell was happening to me?*

He chuckled softly. "You wanted it. *Begged* me for it. We got carried away. I sank so deep inside you that you pleaded with me to never leave. You told me you loved me as I pushed into you over and over and over again. You came so hard for me, Everly. And I came for you."

"Why are you like this?" my voice shook as I absorbed his words, the horror dormant in me but desperately trying to claw its way up.

"Because you're mine as much as you're his."

"I'm not," I whispered, the pain at his words shredding my heart. I had no memory of the things he said. *Did he really control me like that?* "I belong to Raiden."

"For now. But I know something you don't know."

"What?" my voice shook.

"That I'm going to make you feel really good again, and when we're done here, you'll come back for more."

A cry left my lips as his fangs sank into my flesh again, the fog growing denser in my head as he drank from me. Heat swept through me as he held me tightly, my body arching into his. A flurry of tingles shot between my legs as his lips slid down my neck and he bit along my chest at the base of my throat.

I panted, my body growing weaker as the heat grew. I felt like I was going to burst into starlight and moonbeams as his bite took hold and sent me to the moon with so much delicious warmth that I swore to myself I'd never leave his lap as long as he continued to make me feel the way he was in that instant.

In Nevron Blackburn's bite, nothing else mattered. He consumed me. He invaded my thoughts, erasing everything but the space we currently occupied.

"Let go. Stop fighting it," he growled, his lips red with my blood and his eyes bright. He squeezed me hard. *"Just let me in."*

"Nev. Don't. . . *please*. . ."

This was my punishment for betraying Dyre. I knew it was. *What would be my punishment for betraying my heart? My soul? Raiden?*

He let out a snarl and sank his fangs back into me as I fought to hold onto the last tiny shred of control I had left. One slip in front of Nevron was like tumbling forever, him guiding my flailing body as I tried to stop myself.

He dug his fangs in deeper as tiny stars dotted my vision and my last bit of control slipped away from me.

The only thing I could do was enjoy the fall.

RAIDEN

I didn't make it home until the sun was up, opting to spend some time alone at my mother's crypt with a bottle of booze.

I turned down my healing abilities and just let the alcohol course through me, numbing all my pain and worries. I stumbled in at sunrise and made a beeline for Ever's room.

"Ever?" I slurred, frowning at her empty bed. I scrubbed my hand over my face and focused on her in my head.

"Where are you?"

She stirred beneath my call, but the connection was fuzzy. It was probably from all the alcohol in my body.

"I'll be there in a minute."

She snapped off the connection, and I sank onto her bed and put my head in my hands.

I had a brother. A twin. He was dead.

I swallowed, hating I'd been lied to my whole life. I was confused about the predictions and finding my twin. *How could I find him if he was dead?* And an infant at that. It made little sense. I'd been over it and over it all night long.

Add to it that I was at my wits' end over making sure Ever was safe from all the monsters in the world. . .

I rubbed my eyes just as Ever appeared in the room, her hair windswept from her shadow melding.

"Raiden. We have to talk," she said, breathless, as she dropped to her knees before me. "I screwed up."

"What?" I mumbled, blinking at her.

Her brows crinkled. "Are you. . . *drunk?*"

"Sorry. I had a bad night. What's wrong? What's going on?"

She shook her head, her frown deepening. "I'll tell you later. You need to rest or whatever it is you do to fix yourself. You've been up all night. Sleep, OK?" She rose to her feet, but I reached out and grasped her wrist.

"Don't go." I stood and gazed down at her. "Shower with me? I'll get the alcohol out of my system and wake up. Then we can talk."

She hesitated for a moment before finally nodding. I followed her into her bathroom and stripped my clothes off, watching her do the same. In moments, we were bared to one another, the warm water already running in the shower.

She stepped beneath the spray, and I followed, gathering her into my arms, her back to my front.

I pressed a kiss to her bare shoulder and focused on letting my healing energy eat away at the alcohol in my veins. The fog slowly lifted, my thoughts becoming clearer.

"Talk to me," I whispered, kissing her neck. "What happened?"

"I-I have to. . . confess something."

"What?" I turned her around to face me, my heart in my throat.

Was this it? Was she going to tell me she was in contact with Cipher and was choosing them over me? Over Conexus? Over saving the damn world?

"The night I went to Nev." She licked her lips. "T-The night Damien and Brandon went and got me, I, um. . . I. . ."

"What?" I cradled her face, sending out a silent prayer she wasn't about to break my damn heart.

"I h-had sex with him," her voice cracked and tears leaked from her eyes. I stared down at her, my pulse roaring in my ears. "I don't remember doing it. I-I thought we just kissed and made out a little. I-I don't even know why I'm telling you now. I'm so confused. . ."

My hands shook on her face as I gazed down at her. "That's not true. You wouldn't do that."

She sniffled. "I saw him last night. On my patrols. We. . . talked. He-he told me what he did. He has a power to erase memories and change them like Eric does. He's a *sifter* like Eric. I'm sorry. I-I didn't know. I'm so dizzy and confused. I feel like I could sleep forever, but I had to tell you. It's important you know."

I let my hands fall away from her. She reached for me, but I backed up against the wall, my head a damn mess inside as I sifted through my memory of our first time together.

"No," I growled. "No. It's not true."

"Raiden—"

"It's *not* true, Everly. He's crossed a line. I'm sure he played with your mind. I don't know why, but I know without a doubt I was your first."

She reached for me again. I melded away from her so fast her fingers simply slid through my shadow. When I materialized, I was in my room. I dressed quickly and rushed downstairs.

"Where's the fire?" Damien called out around a mouthful of cereal from the couch.

Adam and Jared sat forward.

"Damien. Eric," I shouted.

Eric came into the room holding a muffin. "Yeah?"

"Come with me."

I didn't miss the look of worry they shot at one another as Ever descended the stairs, her hair still wet, dressed in nothing but a hoodie and sweatpants.

"Raiden, talk to me," she pleaded, rushing to me and taking my hand.

I pulled my hand away from hers, my anger at a dangerous boiling point.

"Gen, man, What's going on?" Jared rose to his feet, Adam beside him.

I stared down at Ever, my heart beating so hard I thought it would burst out of my chest. Tenderly, I brushed a tear off her cheek.

"He will pay for this," I said, backing away from her.

"Raiden. No. Don't go. Don't leave! You can't face him like this. You're too angry. You'll do something you'll regret. That I'll regret. Please. Just. . . stay. I-I need you."

Swallowing down my emotions, I took her trembling hand in mine and pressed my lips to her engagement ring. "I'll be back." I flicked my wrist and engulfed her in a thin veil of magic. She made to step out of it but couldn't get past the barrier.

"How did you do that. . . ?" Damien murmured amid the soft gasps in the room.

Sloane, Chloe, and Amanda swept into the room.

"Watch her. She doesn't leave here. Got it?" I didn't think she'd be able to escape my spell anyway. I wasn't even sure where it came from. I just knew what I wanted and focused on it, then it happened. It was probably one of many things I would discover I could do as her Reever. A protection charm, really. A strong one.

They nodded, their eyes wide with confusion. I summoned Mason and Brandon in my mind. They popped into existence almost immediately.

"I need all of you with me. Girls stay behind. We'll be back."

"Raiden," Ever called out as I strode to the door, my guys behind me without question, her fists banging against the barrier. "Raiden! Don't!"

Her calling my name faded away as we left the house.

RAIDEN

"Are you sure?" Eric ventured after I relayed everything to them through our telepathy.

"He didn't do it," I snarled. "He's lying to her, and I want to know why."

"How do you know he's lying?" Adam asked as we stalked through the campus. "I mean, she was pretty distraught early on. And she went to him—"

"Because she bled for me," I rasped, hating to divulge details of our intimate relationship. "I was her first. Not him."

"It didn't look like sex to me," Damien said. "They had their clothes on for the most part when we got there."

"Yeah, Ever's shirt was undone, but that's it. She had a bra and bottoms on." Brandon cast me a quick look and winced. "But is this really Conexus business? I don't want to be that guy, but this seems more like a jealous Reever boyfriend thing than something we should all get our asses kicked by the Order for. No offense, Gen, but I'm not interested in chilling in a Xanan dungeon this weekend and being docked pay."

I stopped my march and turned to my group.

"I understand your concerns, but it's Conexus business at the heart of it. We suspect Blackburn and Ambrose of their involvement with Cipher. Nevron is related to Aviram, the leader of the Cipher. It's too coincidental. This is a seed. I'm killing it before it sprouts. He's up to something. Things weren't right with Ever when she told me." I turned and went straight to Blackburn's dorm and pounded on his door. She shouldn't have been confused about it. I knew sifting. I'd seen Eric do it before. People came out exactly how they'd gone in, only with details changed. Ever was far too conflicted.

Blackburn opened the door right before I was ready to tear it off the hinges. His blond hair was a mess, but he looked like he was refreshed.

I shoved his door so hard it bounced off his shoulder as I stomped into his space.

"What do I owe the pleasure?" he asked mildly, not a bit of concern radiating from him.

I fisted my hands around his shirt and shoved him against the wall and glared at him.

"Why did you tell Everly she did shit she didn't do?"

"Because she needed to know the truth. I care about her enough for her to know," he answered without hesitation.

"But yet you got into her head to erase the memory of it?"

"Only because I didn't want her upset. She was hysterical after we did it. She regretted it. I hated to see her hurt like that, so I altered the memory."

My throat burned with that damn hunger I couldn't figure out. Now wasn't the time to be fighting that shit too. I forced myself to focus on Blackburn.

"You lie."

"Do I? Did she tell you where she was last night? All night?" He raised a brow at me.

I frowned, still holding him. "She was on patrols—"

"Until she found me." He smirked.

My fury was mixed with a new emotion. *Fear.*

I ground my teeth for a moment before I called for Adam. "You patrolled with Ever last night, right?"

"I, uh, did. For a bit. But then Chloe got back and Ever said she could handle it on her own—"

I slammed Nev back against the wall, my anger taking over.

"What did you do to her last night? Did you touch her? Did you get inside her head?" I'd kill him this time. If he hurt her. Touched her. Anything.

"I did everything she asked me to do and then some," he said in a soft, smug voice. *"Shadow."*

I released him and backed away, the world around me fuzzy. How did he know? No one was supposed to know. He hinted at it before, but here he was, outright saying it to me.

"She didn't tell me if that's what you're thinking. I figured it out on my own. You didn't try to cover it very hard," Nev said conversationally as he adjusted his shirt. "I just followed the breadcrumbs. Pieced it together on my own."

I clenched my jaw at his words. This was a disaster. Aviram's family knew who she was. Who I was.

"Tell me what you did to her," I hissed out. "I have no problem taking you to Xanan and forcing it off your forked tongue."

"I told her the truth. I did what I had to do to get her to see. You'll thank me later. I'm not your enemy, Hawthorne."

"You sure as hell aren't my friend."

He nodded. "I could be. I mean, if you'd stop being a dick and pull your head out of your ass. We could all live in a better world."

"A world led by blood thirsty vamps?" I scoffed. "Never going to happen."

"It's what she wants. You know it is." He fixed his bright, blue-eyed gaze on me.

"What did you do to her last night? Don't lie to me, Blackburn. I've seen your eyes like this before. When you fed from her in my office after healing her from the vamp attack." My heart was in my throat as I denied what I feared.

"Make your guys leave, and we'll have a little chat."

I studied him for a moment before I took a step back. "Leave us."

"Man, I don't think we should leave you two alone," Damien started, stepping forward.d

"*Leave. Us.*"

Without another word, they left, the door clicking closed behind them but not before Eric cast me a fearful look.

"Talk, *vamp.*"

He chuckled and moved past me to his fridge and pulled out a bottled water and drank from it. My patience was wearing thin.

"I spent the night with her," he said easily. "She told me you two are engaged. Of course, that didn't stop her from sitting on my lap."

"Mother fu—" I surged forward, the magic burning through my veins as all sorts of ideas on how to torture him raced through my mind.

"Easy, General. Or Shadow. You want to know this or not?" He cocked his head at me as I slowed my attack. I steadied my breathing and waited for him to say something useful. Time was ticking. I wouldn't be able to fight off my feelings for much longer.

"I saw the ring. Rubies are a favorite of vampires. I find it interesting you've chosen them to be her wedding ring."

"They were my mother's favorite," I snarled, watching as he moved to his couch and sat down. He rested his arms over the back cushions and gave me a smile.

"My mother's too. Of course, she was married to my father, so I suppose that was natural for her to be drawn to the gem. But what I found intriguing was the fact that you, someone known for your hatred of vampires, put *our* stone on her finger. Care to divulge that little secret?"

"No," I snapped. "I have no secrets. I've said my piece. My mother loved them. It's in honor of her."

"Your mother. A fae. A psy. Not vampire." He nodded and clicked his tongue. "*Weird.*"

"We aren't here to discuss this shit. We're here because you touched what's mine. I want to know what you did to her and why you did it. I want the truth, Blackburn. I don't want to have to hurt you to get it."

"You want the truth? Fine." He sat forward and rested his elbows on his thighs. "I think you know she's up to something, and it scares the shit out of you. You're worried you're going to lose her to the Cipher. You think *I'm* Cipher. In fact, you think you know everything, don't you? Raiden Hawthorne, Prince of Specials, Conexus General, First-Class Elite. . . knows. . .all." He sat back, his bright blue eyes locked on me. "But you don't know this."

"Then tell me," I snapped, sick of his games. "I don't want a monologue, Blackburn. I want the truth. I want to know what you did to Everly. I don't care about this other shit you're trying to spread."

"Why won't you listen? Why? The fate of our world—my entire race—is at stake here, and you can't stand to listen to anything but your damn self."

"You have five seconds to tell me what I want to know before I call my men in here and we take you to Xanan where I will get the answers I want. What. Did. You. Do. To. Everly?"

He scoffed and got to his feet, shaking his head. "She's working for me. With me. You're right on that account, but I am not Cipher like you'd like to believe. I *hate* Cipher. I'd give my life if it meant they were eradicated from our world. They are a group created by someone within the Order to overthrow your father. We are being blamed for what your people are doing. It's a bait and switch, Hawthorne. And you're carrying out everything they want. You're killing the good guys. Ever knows this. She joined me to save the world." He drew in a deep breath as I rolled his words over in my mind. They struck a chord with me, but I needed more information before I could make my decision. "I know you're her Reever. We need you with us. If you're divided, it could bring so much bloodshed. If she's in the hands of the order, if you both are, our world is screwed. With you in control, you could be the whisper in her ear to drive her to her madness. We need the Mancer and the Reever together. If you fail her, Hawthorne, the task will fall to me. I don't want it to be me because I will not stop until I take down every Order member who has had a hand in killing my people. That means you if you keep on the path you're on. That means her if the Order sinks their claws into her."

I surveyed him in shock. I expected a lot of things, but I didn't expect that.

"So I did what I had to do to her last night," he continued softly. "I told her the truth. She was with me first. I was her first, so that I could be her last. I can't help if you don't like the truth. There's a prophecy that needs to be fulfilled, and I'll be damned if I let you or anyone else stop it from happening. If you're as good as you claim, you'll join me. If you're not, then we'll see each other in hell."

I melded from where I stood to directly in front of him. He didn't flinch away from me as we stood glaring at one another, eye to eye. No one fucking threatened me.

"Aviram, *your family*, has Cipher ties. We've been investigating it for years. You are a liar like the other vamps are. It's your nature to deceive. You will stay away from Everly. Do you understand me? If I see you near her, I will kill you on sight. I don't care who witnesses it." I backed away from him. "She is no longer part of your little group. Don't ruin her life because yours is ending."

"Leaving me to my freedom only tells me you might believe me," he said, his jaw quivering. "That you might need me. We're all running out of time, and you know it. You're no closer to finding the snake in your midst now than you were when you started. Tick tock, Hawthorne. It's not just the fate of the world at stake. It's Everly too."

"I will not join you," I rasped, going to the door. I didn't want to admit that maybe there was something in his words that kept me from hauling him to Xanan. That stopped me from just removing his head from his body. "I meant what I said. Stay away from her and stay out of her head. I had mercy on you today because I know Everly gives a damn about you. You won't always get my mercy."

I stepped out and slammed his door behind me and let out a breath.

"What happened?" Eric demanded, the guys moving toward me.

"We need to have a meeting. Now."

EVERLY

I stood in the veil of magic Raiden left behind as the girls sat on the couch. My mind was racing a mile a minute. The last few weeks had been brutal, and it only seemed to be escalating. I knew I should have just stayed away from Nev, but I couldn't blame it all on him. He was a vampire. It was his nature to drink. I was so desperate for him to trust me again that I'd made a terrible choice that may very well get him killed. I'd never forgive myself if something happened to him. Despite my anger at him for taking it too far once more, he still mattered to me. If my grandmother trusted him, then I trusted him. What I didn't trust was myself. The guilt of falling asleep on his couch after being bitten had left me feeling so guilty I'd ran to Raiden. Finding out I'd been with Nev that one night made me so sick to my stomach I wasn't sure how to traverse those feelings except be honest about them to Raiden. My head was fuzzy, though. I couldn't quite place my thoughts. Where I should have been worried, I was only confused. And these feelings. . . god. I didn't know what the hell they were.

Raiden and I said no secrets. I was trying, and it was going to get someone killed. Getting my shit together was top priority now.

Raiden would have no choice but to punish me for going to Nev last night. I knew it. I'd tied his hands.

"What happened?" Sloane asked, cutting into my thoughts. "Raiden was pissed."

"Yeah, like, did you two fight or something?" Amanda sat forward. "Because it's OK if you did. We know you two get heated with one another. Is Raiden still upset over Nev?"

"I don't know," I whispered. "I screwed up again."

"It's OK. We all do," Sloane said gently. "Raiden is fair. You know he is, and he loves you. He has the guys with him. They're great at keeping his anger in check. I can check in with Damien if you want."

I breathed out and nodded, needing to make sure everything was OK but too scared to ask myself.

Sloane went quiet, her head cocked as she reached out to Damien.

"What's going on?" Amara asked, coming into the room. She flipped her red hair over her shoulder and lifted a brow at me. "Why are you caged in magic? Trying to screw up someone else's life?"

"Yes," I said, my voice barely above a whisper.

She frowned at my response. "Where's Raiden?"

"Dealing with Nevron," Chloe said.

Amara rolled her eyes. "*More* drama? How many times are you going to break his heart before he realizes he left something amazing for something so. . .gross." Her gaze flicked over me, her lip turned up into a sneer.

"It wouldn't matter if he realized anything," Chloe snapped. "He took the Vow of Eternity. Ever owns him until she draws her last breath. You know that. Stop your shit, Amara."

"Even you agree about his realizing it." Amara shot me a wicked smile as she turned away from Chloe to look at me. "Everyone knows it, Ever."

I sucked in a sharp breath as her voice broke into my thoughts.

"You should do him a favor and kill yourself. Just die so he can live a good life and the rest of us won't have to fight your damn battle. You're making him miserable. I'll even help you if you need it. I'll give you the knife. Seems like you like those."

I flung her out of my mind so fast she stumbled back, her cheeks growing crimson.

Amanda let out a squeak as Amara stepped on her foot.

"Everyone is to gather at Conexus house for an emergency meeting. We'll be there in a minute," Eric's voice sounded out in my head before fading off to the silence once more.

"Damien said Raiden didn't hurt Nev. They're on the way back." Sloane swallowed. "Ever, Damien said Raiden is livid. I don't know what went down with you guys, but just be patient, OK? He's given up a lot—"

The door burst open, silencing her.

Raiden swept in first, followed by everyone else. He moved straight for me, his eyes locked on mine. My heart jumped into my throat at his fast approach. He didn't dissipate the barrier. He stepped right through it and flicked his wrist again, silencing everyone around us with another spell.

"They can't hear us and likewise," he said, cradling my face. "I don't believe him. I think he's trying to get into your head. He knows I'm Shadow. He wants me to join whatever the hell he's doing. He didn't come out and say it, but I'm guessing he put a curse on you and anyone else in his little gang who might talk. Or had someone cast on you, and if I had to guess, that's Ambrose's work. But Ever, I'm not joining him. Something isn't right."

"Raiden, please—"

"And you won't join him either. If we're going to save the world, we'll do it alone before we join his side. He's too suspicious. Even if he's right, then we'll fight from another side. I don't have enough information to just join up with him. I can try to uncurse you, but it might make things worse since I don't know exactly what spell he used on you."

"You said you'd go where I go—"

"And I will if I have all the information. Right now, I don't. I need to look into it further and you need to stay away from him until I get it sorted. OK?"

I nodded wordlessly.

"I love you," he murmured. "Promise me, Everly."

"Promise," I whispered, the nausea sweeping through me.

"We'll talk more later. Let's get to the meeting." He didn't wait for me to answer. He waved his barrier spell away. The chattering of Conexus surrounded us. Raiden took my hand and led me to his velvet chair. He sat and nodded for me to take a seat on the arm. I perched beside him, wondering what he was going to do now.

He cleared his throat and silence fell on the room. "Eric and Damien have briefed you by now I'm sure about the Blackburn. . . situation."

I hung my head as he continued.

"We don't know what he's planning or if he's truly Cipher. We're at the same place we've been at. What I know is this. He knows I'm Shadow and Everly's Reever. He knows she's the Mancer. And he's definitely not innocent, whether it's because he's in bed with the Cipher or he's branched off to do something else."

He paused and cast a look around the room. In that moment, he looked so powerful it made my chest clench. He was a king in the making. So beautiful. So. . . lethal. Goosebumps raced over my body.

"He has powers we didn't know he possessed," he continued. "He can control and befuddle the mind. Replace memories. Alter them. Who knows what else. He's a sifter, like Eric. He's a psy vamp, something quite rare. Since Everly is our best source of information on him, she's going to tell you what she knows."

I glanced at him, my lips parted. He wanted me to tell them about everything I knew about Nev?

"Ever?" He watched me, waiting for me to do something.

I licked my lips. "I, uh, I don't know—"

"You dated him. You have to know something," Brandon said.

Right. I couldn't just say that was a lie too. Damnit.

"Raiden is right. Nev is really good with mind stuff, and not just altering. He's cunning too. His psy abilities give him an edge. He's so powerful he can heal bites given by other vampires. If my suspicions are correct, I think he can even change people without harm coming to them."

There was a collective intake of breath at my words. It was just a suspicion, but I wasn't having any doubts on it. I knew Nev could change people without batting a lash.

"He can create new vampires?" Jared winced. "That's not good. They're typically born, not made."

"A vampire hasn't been made in centuries. At least one that has survived long enough to be called a vamp. They usually die as fledglings." Damien sat forward in his chair. "Gen, this could be bad, man."

"It could be," Raiden murmured.

"You actually trust her?" Amara called out. "After you saw what she did with him in the power exchange we did? You saw her, Raiden!"

"We all make mistakes," Raiden snapped at her. "It's not any of your business anyway, Amara. You don't know the story, so I advise you to keep your thoughts to yourself."

She glared at him, a muscle popping along her jaw as her glare shifted to me.

"Amara," Raiden warned.

It only took me a moment to realize he was conversing with her using telepathy. She quieted and looked at a spot over my head as they ended their conversation and he spoke again.

"Everly. Continue."

"I-I don't know much more than that."

Amara scoffed.

"Anything at all is helpful, Ever," Eric said, his voice gentle.

I bit my bottom lip and decided I was just going to say it.

"Nev isn't Cipher. Many of you said you'd follow me wherever I went. I'm telling you Nev is the way—"

"Everly," Raiden called out. "No."

"Raiden wants more information," I pushed. "If he gets it, if I can prove Nev is being truthful, will you believe me, then? Will you follow me? You guys know someone in the Order is doing this stuff. You may not like vampires, but they're just like us. That's like me saying I don't like shifters because I hate animals. They aren't all the same and they aren't all bad. I'm asking you guys to trust me. Please."

"You tried to kill our general," Amara snarled, getting to her feet.

"Tried to murder him in our home! Why would we trust you? You're screwing Nev behind Raiden's back, running back to him when you should be on patrols, and now this? No. This is ridiculous." She looked out wildly at everyone before plowing on. I could feel Raiden tense beside me as I shifted on the arm of the chair. "As fourth in line, I make a motion that Everly Torres be taken before the Order to be punished for her involvement with a suspected Cipher member. If our general doesn't take her to the dungeons himself, I will get my father involved. I'll win." Her chest heaved as she glared at me.

"You're out of line, Mara," Raiden seethed, getting to his feet.

"Gen, she's right," Adam called out. He threw me an apologetic look. "You should punish Everly. In the dungeons. If she goes before the Order, you know it could be worse. What if. . .you know, the traitor is there and tries to harm her? It has to be you. Amara isn't going to back off. I think it's best for Ever if you just do it."

"He's right," I said, standing up. It sucked and it hurt, but it was the only way. "I accept the punishment. We have more important things to do than sit around and argue. So if I must be punished in the dungeons, so be it. I will not fight it."

"It's not happening. I've already taken you to the dungeons for punishment. I will not punish you twice. As for you, I want you to go sit in my office and wait for me." The look Raiden gave Amara sent chills down my spine. "I'll deal with you later."

She stormed out of the room and slammed his office door behind her. Raiden flung a silence charm after her. It blanketed the entire wall, closing her off from us.

He sat back in his seat and pulled me onto his lap.

"Continue," he breathed out, giving me a squeeze.

I looked at my hands. I had nothing else I could say about Nev, so I went with an ugly truth about myself.

"I can raise the dead," I whispered. "I know I did it with Eric. I don't think I'd have been able to if it hadn't been for trying it on someone else before."

"What?" Mason murmured.

"Where did you get a dead body to try on?" Brandon demanded.

"When?" Damien said.

"Oh, gross." Amanda visibly shuddered and wrapped her cardigan tighter around herself.

I swallowed. "The night I came back and was covered in mud. Raiden, you asked me what I'd been doing. I was in the cemetery digging up Basil Hessen."

He stiffened beneath me as the room lit with roars of surprise, disgust, and intrigue.

"How, my sweet Mancer, were you able to get outside the grounds to the cemetery? I don't even let you out there for patrols."

"I was afraid. I wanted to make sure I could do it in case it happened. I-I melded there."

"How did you know where to find his grave? His specifically?" Damien asked.

"I-I just knew," I offered weakly, not wanting to divulge how I knew.

"So you just brought a shovel and started digging in the middle of the cemetery, alone, at night?" Sloane shivered. "Girl, what the actual hell?"

"What happened?" Raiden asked in a low voice.

"I didn't know what I was doing. I touched his head first. Nothing. I was just about ready to give up when I went for his chest. The strangest sensations came over me. I actually was getting out to call it a night when he came back to life."

"A corpse? Like a rotting corpse?" Chloe gagged.

"Yeah. It wasn't fun," I muttered. "I got scared and ran. That's how I got so muddy. I fell and rolled down the hill and ended up spraining my ankle. He caught me eventually. I-I thought I was going to die, but he-he showed me things."

"What things?" Raiden demanded.

I licked my lips, remembering the words Basil choked out to me.

"One of two

The Second.

The Other.

Same Father. Same Mother.

One of shadow.

One of blood.

Brought together

When evil floods.

One side.

And the other.

Always apart.

Forever brothers.

Rule of Five will survive.

In her death, the blood will rise.

A new king will be crowned.

The time is five.

Fear not her death

For it is her wrath that should be tamed

One life gone, she has another

And in it, she shall be named.

Queen of Shadow.

Queen of Light.

Forever and Never

Fear her fight.

One side will lose

Another will win.

The true victory

Depends on Her whim

The Queen of the Dead comes for all."

I let out a shuddering breath before finishing the words Basil spoke. "You choose. Everly Torres, Queen of the Dead." I looked to Raiden. "Declan Eres was the last person alive to hear Basil's prediction. You killed him in an interrogation. I had to get the answers," my voice cracked as I got to my feet and faced Raiden. "You killed him, Raiden."

"He was Cipher," he said gently.

"You don't know who is Cipher these days. You'll never know if you don't listen."

"Everly." Raiden got to his feet and cradled my face. "I saw him kill a Nattie. A natural. Like your mom and Nina. He ripped her throat out. I took him into custody despite wanting to end him on the spot. He died in interrogation. When I tell you he was Cipher, please believe me."

"Ever, he really was," Eric cut in from his seat. "Damien and I were with Raiden when it happened. The girl was just a child. Twelve at the most. The Nattie news reported it as an animal attack, but we know it was him. Raiden tried to save her but she was already gone by the time we got him off her."

But Nev said Declan was Dyre, not Cipher. I shook my head, more confused than ever.

"Is that all he said? Basil?" Raiden asked gently.

I nodded. "Y-Yeah. He went back to being dead after that."

Raiden studied me for a moment. "OK. Well, that prophecy is actually interesting to hear. Everyone has talked of it for many years and the fact you did that. . ." He shook his head. "Sit?"

I took his hand and let him lead me back to his chair. He pulled me back down onto his lap.

"I drank a lot last night," he started. "I didn't come home. I sat in the royal crypt beside my mother's coffin."

I frowned and looked over at him. No one said a word as he breathed out.

"I gave my report to the Order, then I spoke with my father privately. I gave him news he wasn't happy about." He grew quiet for a moment before continuing. "He must have felt like having some bonding time with me because he decided to divulge some ugly family secrets."

"Oh shit," Chloe said, her eyes widening. Everyone shifted, either learning forward or cocking their heads.

"My father divulged to me that I was a twin at birth."

The silence was deafening at Raiden's words.

"What?" Eric called out, his brows crinkled.

"You have a twin?" Adam looked at Chloe who stared wide-eyed at Raiden.

"How did you not know you had a twin?" Mason said.

"Wait, was it a girl?" Damien asked. "Because where is she?"

"It was a brother," Raiden said calmly. "He died during childbirth. Kazimir Wesley Hawthorne. I was five minutes older. My father never saw his body. He said he wanted to focus on what he had, not on what he lost. My mother took Kazimir's body to be buried in her hometown. Father did not go. I went with my mother. They laid my brother to rest in a family crypt there."

"I'm so sorry," Sloane said, breaking another silence that had fallen.

Raiden nodded but said nothing.

"Wait. If you're the Reever and this prophecy speaks of a brother you have. . .just how?" Damien frowned as he stared at Raiden. "Is Ever supposed to go to your brother's grave and dig him up and-and bring him back?"

"Oh no," Amanda whimpered. Brandon reached out and gave her hand a squeeze.

"What good would an animated baby do?" Mason piped up. "I mean, babies can't think or talk. There's something else there."

"Where did you say he's buried?" Eric asked.

"Ravenvale Grove. Outside London," Raiden said. "It's a Special village. Or town. It was back then. I did look at it on the map today. It's grown quite large since then, tripling in population. It's a popular safe place for all kinds."

"Which means bad kinds hang there," Chloe grumbled.

Raiden nodded. "Likely."

"So what's the plan, Shadow?" Adam asked. "I know you have one."

I studied Raiden as he stared at the floor, his arm around my waist. He looked so hurt and confused, I just wanted to pull him in for a hug. Having the truth kept from him like that for so many years had to have devastated him.

"I'd like to go to London. I'll need Eric and Damien. Everyone else can stay here—"

"I'm not letting you go alone," I broke in. "I'm going too."

"It's not safe for you," he said, sighing.

"I'm safest with you. London is too far away for you to just flit back to me here. If something happens, I'm toast. The way Amara was looking at me tonight makes me think I'm already burned toast."

"I agree. Ever needs to go. We'll keep an eye on her. Besides, if one of us gets gutted in the damn place, we'll need her to bring us back." Eric winked at me. I offered him a small smile in return.

"I vote bring her. I'm too pretty to die," Damien said, slapping his knees. "Right, Sloane?"

"Right."

He gave her a double take. She offered him a quick smile that had his grin widening.

"Fine. She comes with us, but we have to protect her. We can portal to Xanan and then portal jump from there. Everyone else will remain on campus."

"Will Amara be in charge?" Sloane asked, wincing. "She is fourth."

"She won't be after tonight. Brandon and Adam are next in line. They'll be in charge. We will have phones on us so you'll be able to reach us through the distance." Raiden paused. "I don't have to tell you how important this is to keep quiet. I don't even want Amara to know where we're going. She's angry right now and may make some choices she'll regret. So as far as any of you know, we're off doing something I never divulged. Got it?"

Everyone murmured their agreement.

"When are you leaving?" Mason asked.

"I think first thing in the morning would be best. We need the answers so we can make our next move. For now, let's get some rest. I want everyone's ears to the ground. If you hear anything about Blackburn, I need to know about it. You guys know the drill. I'll see you all tomorrow. Or not."

I moved off his lap and he stood. Everyone else rose and began shuffling off, chattering amongst themselves.

"I'll see you later, OK?" He thumbed my bottom lip.

I nodded, worry alive and well within me.

"Be in my bed. I'll be up as soon as I'm done dealing with this."

By this I knew he meant Amara.

"Will you be OK?" I asked.

He scoffed. "From a werewolf? *Please.* She's one word away from a transfer out of here."

"She's hurting, Raiden."

His face darkened. "We all hurt sometimes. What she's doing isn't right."

"Not everyone reacts to pain the same. She makes me so mad too, but I get it."

"That makes one of us."

"Be kind to her. Just. . . not too kind."

He leaned in and placed a gentle kiss on my lips. "My kindness is reserved for you alone, my love."

He pulled away from me and made his way to his office. His usual tall, strong stature looked tired and tense. I knew he was stressed. Amara was only adding to it. In a way, I hoped he transferred her just so he could get some peace.

But knowing Amara, that would be the last thing she'd give if he transferred her. It would probably be the beginning of another fire we'd struggle to contain.

RAIDEN

"Took you long enough," Amara grumbled from her seat next to the fire.

I said nothing and went straight for the tarish and poured myself a glass. I threw it back before pouring another.

"You never used to drink so much," she commented, glaring at me from her chair.

"Trust me, I did," I muttered, walking toward her. "I used to protect you from seeing it. Or maybe I was protecting myself."

She scowled at my answer as I settled in my chair beside hers, a small table between us. The fire crackled merrily in the fireplace, casting a dim orange glow around the room. The heat was nice, but all I really wanted to do was go upstairs and curl up next to Ever and shove all the shit out of my head. I knew she wasn't telling me everything, and I'd be lying if I said it didn't hurt. I also knew that she probably couldn't.

On the other hand, I didn't want to know it. What she did last night didn't matter in the grand scheme of things. I knew Blackburn was up to something and Ever was caught in the crossfire. Anything she did was her way of trying to smooth over their damaged relationship. One I was trying my hardest to squash out before bad shit happened.

Because it would. Because Blackburn really was as cunning as Ever said.

I was her Reever. Her protector. I needed to keep her away from him. I'd do everything in my power to make that happen.

"What's my punishment?" she asked as she stared into the embers.

"I'm going on a mission with Eric and Damien in the morning. I'm taking Everly with me. I'm leaving Adam and Brandon in charge in my absence."

"I'm fourth—"

"You're suspended until I get back. If you behave yourself while I'm gone, I'll consider your reinstatement."

"You can't do that. All I was doing was suggesting what everyone else was afraid to say—"

"You knew I made her stay in the dungeons already. You knew she was already punished for her involvement with Blackburn. What you were really doing was making this so much harder than it has to be."

She pursed her lips.

"I meant what I said, Mara. I want our friendship to remain intact. I understand you're upset—"

"You broke my heart," she whispered. "I love you so much and you don't care anymore. The moment she came into your life, you changed."

"We've been over this, Mara. So many times. Everly is who I'm meant to be with."

"Fated mates," she muttered. "It's an old wives' tale."

"It exists. Blessed by the stars. Some people are lucky for it. Others aren't. I'm sorry about that. I really am. I want your happiness, but you have to want it to or it'll never work. I'll end up having to transfer you out of here."

"My father would be so disappointed with me. He's already furious that I was jilted. He thinks I did something wrong."

I sighed. "I'm sorry. If he can't see what this is, then there isn't anything we can do about it. You need to start looking out for you,

Amara. Don't worry about what I'm doing or what Everly's doing. You. Your failure to fall in line and accept what is will end with your dishonorable discharge from our ranks. You know that carries plenty of long nights in the Xanan dungeons. I don't want that to happen to you. I don't want to send you away. I keep fighting it. I'm running out of fight."

"You know why you won't ever just send me away?" She locked her gaze on me.

"Humor me. Why?"

"Because you know you might need me someday. That I might still be the key to your happiness. You keep me here because you know it's true. I stay here because I know it's true."

"Amara—"

"I promise to be good if you just say it. Just tell me, Raiden. Tell me you don't believe everything she's saying. That you aren't hurting because you know she was with Nev last night doing god knows what with him. He has a reason for everything he does, but so does she. Tell me and I swear I won't act up. I won't fight. I just need to hear it from you."

I swallowed down my drink and looked at my hands. She was right. We both knew it. I hated the ugly little voice in my head screaming it at me.

I sighed. "I don't believe she's telling me everything. I am hurting about the possibilities of last night, but I don't believe she cheated on me. Everly wouldn't. Not now. Now that she's mine and I'm hers. I know her. I know what her love feels like. This is her being as honest as she can. My mission will hopefully shed more light on things. I keep you here because you're a good fighter, not because I'm harboring love for you. Not that kind of love. I care for you and I always will. But love. . . Amara, my love belongs to her. Is that what you wanted to hear?"

She wiped at her eyes. "It's enough. I'll behave."

I frowned at that, figuring she'd have lashed out at me again. I didn't care, though. I was over dealing with this and exhausted. "We have a deal?"

"Yes."

I got to my feet. "Good. I'll see you when I return. Please remember this conversation."

"I wouldn't dream of forgetting it." She didn't elaborate, and I didn't give a shit. The only thing I cared about was getting upstairs to my girl.

EVER WAS CUDDLED up in my bed when I got upstairs. Despite the darkness, I could still feel her eyes trained on me as I stripped out of my clothes, opting to just wear my boxers to bed. I crawled in beside her and gathered her to me and pressed a kiss to her bare shoulder.

"Is everything OK?" she asked softly.

"For now. That's good enough for me. I can't be assed with it at the moment. I have more important things to be concerned with."

"Like what I did last night," she whispered.

I swallowed, not saying a word. She turned in my arms to face me.

"Raiden, I-"

"I don't need to know."

"You do. We said no secrets. Some I-I can't divulge, but this one I can. I wanted Nev to trust me again. After everything that happened, I was afraid of losing his friendship. His trust. His. . . loyalty. I want to free people. I want there to be peace. I believe in more, but fear what it means. We don't want to fight this alone. We need him, Shadow."

"We don't, baby," I answered, resting my forehead against hers. "You have me."

"I know I do. But I need him too. Something deep inside me says he's important to all of this. I have to trust that. We're in over our head. I was afraid of losing the trust I'd built with him. So I-I offered my blood to him."

I closed my eyes, my forehead still pressed to hers. Vampires weren't allowed to feed from anyone. They were to get their blood from banks and drink that way. I'd only allowed Blackburn's fangs anywhere near Ever because I needed him to help me close her wounds the night she was injured.

"He gets greedy when he drinks. I know it's wrong, but I wanted to prove to him I could be trusted. Even if everything is wrong, there has to be some right in it somewhere. I need answers. I think he has them."

"He's playing you," I rasped, my hands shaking as I held her. I'd seen how he made her moan in my office when he'd healed her wounds and drank from her. I knew his power over her body.

I asked the question that made my insides twists.

"Did he touch you?"

"I-I don't think so. It wasn't supposed to go so far, but his bite. . ."

"It feels good," I murmured in a thick voice, my throat burning from that strange hunger again. "I know it does. I saw how your body reacted to him when he bit you in my office. Your moaning. . ."

"I-I only want you," she whispered. "I swear it. The feeling though. . . It confuses me so much."

"I wish I could give you that feeling. I'm jealous that I can't. It makes me that much angrier at him. I want to be the one to make you feel good. You're mine. My girl. My Mancer. My queen. The idea he touched you. Tasted you. *Wants* you. . . is driving me insane."

"I won't do it again. I think it worked to gain his trust back."

"It doesn't matter if it worked because I'm not letting you go back to see him. Do you understand? You're everything to me, Everly. What sort of protector would I be if I couldn't keep you safe?" I stared down at her, nothing the fear that flashes quickly over her face. It made my heart clench. Would she defy me? Do it anyway and break my trust in her? The thought made me ill.

"What if he's right, though? What if we need to follow him? Would you? If I left because I believed it, would you really follow?"

I breathed out, hating that this conversation was happening. My fears in her potential actions kicked up a notch. "If the evidence is there to support it, I would follow you to the ends of the earth. I'd follow you anywhere, but I can't follow you to your doom. I'll save you each time I can. I swear it. And I'll love you for always."

"I'll love you for always too," she whispered. "But, Raiden—"

"Promise you're done? Promise we can work on getting answers before you see him again? I need you to promise me, Everly." I swallowed, hoping she'd agree. The fact I had her moaning with his fangs deep inside her skin playing in my mind on repeat left me barely in control. The anger was rising. I needed her to promise me.

"I promise."

I pulled away from her and placed her hand over my heart and then placed my hand over hers. "This means a lot to me." I leaned in and kissed her. "Thank you."

She said nothing, opting to stare at me through the darkness.

"Don't think me some whiny, jealous asshole. I do what I do because I love you with everything I am. We're saving the world. We should be cautious. We can only trust each other right now."

"And Eric and Damien," she added.

I chuckled. "And Eric and Damien."

"I'm sorry. For letting him—"

I silenced her with a kiss. "I don't want to talk about that anymore. It's over."

"OK." Her breath feathered along my lips. "Shadow?"

"Mm?" I asked, running my hand along her side.

"I-If you could bite me and taste me, would you want to?"

My throat burned with her words. I had no idea what this new agony was, but I didn't like it. Before I spoke, I cleared my throat. "I don't hold with vampire fantasies, Everly." My mouth watered, and I inched closer to her neck. "But I'd love to taste you like that."

"Really?"

"Yes," I answered truthfully, ashamed of the feeling of desperation washing over me as my throat tightened, the ache gnawing painfully at me.

"I'd let you."

My heart jumped at the prospect. I pressed my lips to hers as the wild idea of biting her raced through my mind. There was no way in hell I'd bite her. Why would I want to? I wasn't a vampire. I hated vampires. Maybe knowing how good it made her feel made me want to make her feel that way.

Whatever that feeling was, it needed to leave. The hunger at tasting her was growing. Nothing like it had ever happened to me before.

Her fingers tangled in my silver hair, her body flush to mine.

"I never wanted to hurt you. I'll make it up to you," she rasped against my lips as I ran my hands beneath her tank top and cradled her full breast. Her lips trailed along my jaw until she got to my neck and sucked against my flesh. I ran her pebbled bud between my index finger and thumb, desperate to be inside her.

She pushed me onto my back and straddled me before removing her shirt. I stared up at her in wonder as her black hair tumbled around her. Slowly, she moved down my body until she tugged my boxers down my legs and licked along my hard length.

"Everly," I breathed out, my fingers in her hair. She responded by drawing my thickness deep into her mouth.

A soft moan slipped past my lips as her warm mouth sucked me. I tangled my fingers in her hair and moved her head up and down at a pace that made my toes curl.

Within minutes, she had me ready to blow.

"Baby," I rasped. "Y-You don't have to."

Her answer was to suck harder and deeper until I couldn't contain the euphoria any longer. I exploded into her mouth as I shook, her name on my lips and my fingers twisted in her silky locks.

Her suction lessened, and she licked and cleaned me gently as I came down from my high, my body still trembling.

"Come here." I reached for her and hauled her up my body. The moment she was near enough, I pressed my lips to hers and kissed her deeply. She moved against me, and I wasted no time shoving her pajama bottoms and panties off. With ease, I rolled her onto her back, our lips never breaking apart.

I nudged her legs apart and positioned myself at her entrance and pushed inside. She arched into my body, her soft moan vibrating against my lips as I bottomed out in her.

"Tell me you're mine," I whispered in her ear as I thrust into her.

"I'm yours, Shadow. Always yours."

She raked her fingernails through my hair and down my back, making me desperate to have her heat clenching around me. I picked up my pace, shoving into her over and over amid her soft cries, both of us breathless.

Her body tensed before she quivered, drawing me deep inside her as she tightened around me.

"S-Shadow. Oh god," she moaned as I worked her over. It wasn't until she cried out for me twice more that I spilled myself inside her, both of us covered in a sheen of sweat.

I balanced my weight over her as she gave me a sated smile.

"I love you," she said in a throaty whisper.

"I love you too, baby. Don't forget it."

"Always?"

"Forever," I murmured before kissing her again.

Forever would never be long enough. Not with my Everly.

She was all mine.

EVERLY

*R*aiden took my hand in his as he activated the portal to Xanan in the basement. Going back so soon wasn't something I was looking forward to, but at least I wouldn't be tossed in a dungeon.

"Ready?" He looked over his shoulder at Damien, me, and Eric.

"Let's do this," Damien said. He stuffed his blueberry muffin into his mouth, sending crumbs tumbling down the front of his black gear.

"No manners." Eric dusted crumbs off his own shoulder with a frown as Damien gave me a wink.

Raiden tugged my hand, and I gripped him tightly as we stepped into the portal. The immediate squeeze came, making it hard to expand my lungs as we tumbled through light and shadow.

Raiden kept me upright as we came careening into Xanan, his hand firmly around mine. His aquamarine eyes skirted the area before he checked on Eric and Damien, who just stepped out of the portal. It sealed itself closed, looking like nothing more than an ornate stone archway.

"Come," Raiden instructed, giving my hand a gentle squeeze. I fell in step beside him with Eric and Damien flanking us.

"Quiet this morning," Damien commented as we walked toward the castle.

"Always is this early. Mid-morning is when it really starts picking up," Raiden said.

"How many people are in the city of Xanan?" I asked, looking around. From what I'd gathered, the portal was on castle grounds. It was simply outside its inner walls. I couldn't see past the massive stone castle and its walls.

"Thousands," Eric said. "What was the last count, Shadow?"

"Nearly three hundred thousand."

"What?" I squeaked. I had no idea there were that many people within Xanan. I figured maybe twenty thousand at the most, but over a quarter of a million?

Raiden glanced over to me. "It's the largest city in our world. It's our capital city."

"How does it go so unnoticed?" I pressed as we walked.

"Magic," Damien said, doing a spin as he walked.

"There are barriers set in place. It's like the Conexus house. We can add to it as we need it. It doesn't really impact the exterior, though. It simply adjusts the space within." Eric gave me a smile. "It's physics and a whole lot of what Damien said."

"It's crazy," I muttered.

"It's going to be yours someday." Raiden squeezed my hand. "Our kingdom."

"Aw, listen to him being all sweet," Damien teased.

Raiden pulled my hand to his lips and kissed my knuckles before we got to the gates.

"Your Highness," a guard suited up in all black gear said in a deep voice, his accent the same as Raiden's and the guys.

The gate swung open, and we stepped through onto cobblestone paths. I hadn't seen a lot of this the time I'd been there. Fear had been guiding me. That and an angry Raiden. At least now I could take in what it really looked like.

A massive stone castle with turrets and towers that stretched high into the morning sky. Loads of trees that were bare from the cool winter chill. Had there not been a fresh layer of snow on the ground, I knew I'd have seen sweeping lawns and beautiful flowers.

"This is breathtaking," I said, trying to take in Raiden's home.

Raiden smiled at me. "It's our home. Maybe I'll be able to show you our kingdom when we get back. There are so many wonderful places here I'd love for you to see."

"I'd like that."

"As cute as you two are, we have company," Damien said under his breath.

He was right. A tall, middle-aged man walked toward us in sweeping purple robes, his hair dark with light silver along the sides. Sangrey Hawthorne. Raiden's uncle. I'd met him at Conexus house after I'd gone as a guest on a Conexus haunt mission. It hadn't been a good experience overall.

"Uncle," Raiden greeted him as the man stopped in front of us.

"Raiden. It's good to see you. I didn't get a chance to speak to you after your meeting last time you were here. I am glad you could visit with your father, though."

"Yes, as was I." Raiden cleared his throat. "Uncle, you remember Everly Torres."

"The Mancer." His eyes lit up as he took me in.

Immediately, I snuggled closer to Raiden, my senses tingling. He reached for my free hand and took it, bringing it to his lips, where he placed a kiss on it.

"It is an absolute pleasure to see you again, Everly. Believe me when I say you have my deepest regrets that last time we didn't get a chance to get to know one another."

I gave him a quick smile, the desire to yank my hand back growing by the minute.

"It's nice to see you again," I said, giving him a slight nod of my head as he released my hand. I breathed out, the surge of anxiety dissipating from my body.

His smile widened. "Hispanic, yes?"

"Yes."

"¿Hablas español?"

"Sí, señor."

"Asistí a uno de nuestros institutos en Texas por un breve tiempo en mi juventud. Aprendí español mientras estuve allí. Por supuesto, fue por una hermosa rosa española."

"Mi madre es originalmente de Texas. Ella también conoció a mi padre en la universidad."

"Your mother is Nattie, yes?"

I nodded.

He glanced to Raiden before addressing me in Spanish again.

"Se rumorea que estás comprometida con nuestro príncipe."

I looked to Raiden who raised his brows at me. I knew Raiden wasn't fluent in Spanish, nor were Eric and Damien. Sangrey said there were rumors about Raiden and I being engaged. I wasn't in the mood to talk about all that with him, especially since Raiden couldn't really understand the conversation.

"Quizás esa sea una charla para otro momento, señor."

His smile stretched as he looked to Raiden. "She's smart, this one. And loyal. I like her very much, Raiden."

Raiden smiled. "I like her very much too, Uncle."

"Well, I suppose enough idle chat, though I am definitely enjoying conversing with such a beautiful woman. Are you here to see your father?"

"No. Just passing through. I wanted to take Everly to visit the kingdom."

"Well, if the rumors are true, then I'd say it's important you do that. If you get a chance when you're done, do stop in. Everything has been so busy lately we haven't had much time to talk. And with things going the way they are, I daresay we're due for a chat."

"Of course, Uncle. I cannot guarantee it, but I will try."

"Excellent." He clapped Raiden on the shoulder. "I must be off. I'm due to meet Sir Parsons for coffee this morning before we meet with the Order to go over a few reports of stepping up security at the barriers."

"Have there been creatures spotted? Cipher?" Raiden asked sharply.

"There have been some reports. We've stepped up security a bit, but it wouldn't hurt to add to it. Rather too many than not enough."

"Are you using Conexus?" Eric asked. "Because if you need more manpower for additional spell casting, I'm sure our witches and warlocks wouldn't mind helping."

"We just may. It depends on what the reports say. We do have reports coming in today from the east group as well as south. West was here yesterday. Of course, Raiden gave his report a few days early, which we all appreciate."

"Let me know if you'll need anything, Uncle. We are fully staffed within Dementon grounds. I can lend manpower to the cause here if needed to help strengthen the barriers."

"Yes, of course. Thank you. I'll let you know on that."

Raiden nodded. "We best be going. I'll see you soon, Uncle."

"Have fun. Show her the sweets shop. She looks like a young lady with a sweet tooth." He winked at me.

I gave him a quick smile.

His eyes raked over me as Raiden wound his arm around my waist.

"It was nice seeing you," Damien said, his brows crinkled as he watched Sangrey. He seemed to snap out of his overly long look at me and bid us goodbye once more before walking in the direction we'd come from.

"He was being exceptionally weird," Damien mused, turning to Raiden.

"Guess he was excited," Eric said as we began walking again.

"Excited? He looked like he was hungry and wanted to eat Everly in one bite." Damien let out a little chuckle. "Man, how would you feel if your uncle snagged up your fiancée?"

Raiden let out a soft huff of laughter. "Ever wouldn't leave me for my uncle."

"I don't know. Your uncle has pulled some hot tail before. Ever would be a hell of a prize," Damien continued.

"She's mine," Raiden grunted, placing a fierce kiss on my temple.

"You damn caveman," Damien chortled. "Whatever. But you had to notice the way he was staring at her."

"Everly is a beautiful woman. I'd have stared too." While I knew Raiden was trying to act like it didn't matter, I'd felt the tension in his body when Sangrey looked at me.

"He was kind of creepy," I said, wrinkling my nose. "I'd never leave you for him."

Eric let out a laugh. Damien's grin widened.

"My uncle is a decent man. He was being honest. It really is a pleasure to meet you," Raiden said as we entered the castle through a massive door after the guards moved aside and bowed their heads for him. We were quiet as we walked the length of the hall, our shoes on the polished marble making soft tapping noises as we moved.

We reached a door to the right, and Raiden led us through a doorway. A massive room greeted us on the other side, filled with archways.

"Portal room," Eric said. "We can get to many places in the world from here. It makes things easier."

"Why do we enter on the edge of the grounds, then?"

"That archway was set in place long ago," Raiden answered. "I could enter here, but it notifies the Order since it's inside the castle. Sometimes I'd much rather make a quiet entrance. The outside portal allows me that."

"And when we leave here using one of these? Won't that notify them?"

"Yes, but I won't be here to listen to anyone say anything about it." He shot me a wink which made me smile.

That worked for me.

Raiden pressed his hand to an archway with ruins on it. I couldn't read it before it glowed a brilliant shade of blue. He offered me his hand, the glow illuminating his face. He was so beautiful at that moment that I could only stare at him.

He looked to me, his eyebrows raised and the tiniest of smirks on his plump lips. "Everly?"

I slipped my hand in his and he stepped into the glow, taking me with him. The tugging in my navel grew as we were pulled through the portal, colors, lights, and sounds swirling around us. When we landed, I was more graceful than last time and didn't stumble as we stepped into an unfamiliar landscape. Eric and Damien stepped out behind us.

"Ah, London," Damien said as he dusted off his black jacket and looked around. "My fourteenth favorite place in the world."

Eric chuckled, and Raiden shook his head.

"Where's your favorite place?" I asked.

"Wherever Sloane is," he answered with a small smile.

I grinned at him. "Why don't you tell her that?"

"She'd never believe me." He shrugged, his cheeks tinting pink.

"I think she would if you just said it."

"I agree," Eric said. "You two like one another. I don't know why you keep denying it."

"Because it's just not our time yet."

"Take it from me. You never know just how much time you have. Make the most of it," Eric said softly.

I swallowed hard at his words. His death still had him shaken up. I didn't blame him. Death had a way of putting us in our place.

Damien clapped him on the back but said nothing. I looked around us, taking in the area we stepped out of.

"A tree?" I raised my brows at Raiden. The portal appeared to be a massive oak tree.

"Hyde Park," Raiden said. "It's beautiful here."

"He used to bring Amara here. It's her favorite place to picnic," Damien supplied. I wrinkled my nose, not needing to know that information. I didn't miss the scowl Raiden shot in Damien's direction.

We walked away from the tree and trekked down a path, the chilly air nipping at us. We shimmered so we were undetectable by the Natties. Raiden cast a thin veil of magic around us so we would be warmer. Having three of the biggest bad asses in Conexus at my side offered me some comfort from whatever creatures lurked here. It was afternoon though, so maybe the daylight would keep them at bay. At least I hoped so.

"Do you know where we're going?" I asked as I nervously looked around us. For it being on the chilly side, there were still people milling about.

"Yes," Raiden said. "I have a place not far from here."

"You have a place here?"

He nodded. "I have them throughout the world. Just safe houses and such in the event I need something."

"Don't let him kid you, Ever. He's the damn prince. He has loads of mansions. They aren't safe houses." Damien grinned at Raiden, who gave him another scowl.

"It's true, I do have many places, but I honestly hardly ever stop in to check on them. We're only going to this one so I can get my car."

Raiden never failed to surprise me. I had no idea he had any of this.

"So, Ever," Damien started. "You and Shadow are. . . active, right?"

"Damien," Raiden warned.

"It's OK. I know you are. I'm just going to help you out with a little something," Damien plowed on before I could answer him. "Shadow here likes to bang it out in public. Or at least he would if he could find a girl to do it with—"

Raiden flicked his wrist and Damien's words were cut off by the silence charm that he'd flung at him. I didn't need to hear Damien to know he was calling Raiden an asshole and laughing.

My face grew hot at the thought of Raiden taking me in public. I chanced a look at him to see him give me the side-eye, a tiny smirk on his lips. Whether it was about silencing Damien or his desire for other things, I wasn't sure.

We walked several blocks, Damien still in his bubble of silence.

"This is my first time in London," I said, looking around at everything.

"Yeah?" Raiden glanced at me. "What do you think so far?"

I shrugged. "It's OK."

Eric chuckled. "I prefer Xanan over London. Even Raiden's palace puts Buckingham to shame. It's barely a blip in comparison."

"Does your palace have a name? This one is Buckingham. Yours has to be called something," I said.

"Taegoria Palace." Raiden stopped us in front of a townhouse. "We're here."

He led us forward and waved his hand over the doorknob. The door swung open and we followed him inside.

As far as nice homes went, this place was right up there. With an open floor plan and hardwood floors, it was spacious and airy. Dark, heavy drapes hung on the windows and leather furniture sat in the living room. The kitchen was pristine, with granite countertops and an island.

"Wow," I murmured, looking around. "This is yours?"

"*Ours*," he said, squeezing my hand before he let go and moved to an office situated off the side of the living room.

"Nice, huh? This is one of his smaller models," Eric said.

"Does he come here often?"

"Probably one of his most visited places. I think he enjoys the bustle of the city. Plus, it is fairly close to Xanan."

"Do you know where else he has places?" Aside from the furniture, the place was fairly bare.

"New York City, Paris, Sicily, Rome, Chicago, Los Angeles, Dallas. He has a few in Ireland and Switzerland. I think he has one in Bali, but I've never been to that one. We don't make it that direction often." Eric sank onto the leather sofa as Damien rummaged through the fridge and pulled a bottle of water out.

Damien said something, but we couldn't hear him. He rolled his eyes and flopped onto the stool at the island as Eric let out a soft laugh.

"He has many more, but he'd have to give you all the names," Eric finished.

I nodded, absorbing it all. Before Raiden and Dementon, my mom worked her ass off to afford what little we had. I'd tried to get a job but she wouldn't let me, citing that I needed to focus on school so I could have a better life than we had.

Little did she know I adored our life. She gave me everything I could have ever wanted. I wished I'd have told her that more often.

"What are you thinking about?" Eric murmured.

I shrugged. "Home."

He gave me a sad smile. "Life happens fast, huh?"

"Too fast. I'm going to check on Shadow." I moved away from him, knowing if I took the time to stay, my emotions would overwhelm me. I was going to be a queen. I'd have a kingdom. Houses in every country. A king for a husband. It was beginning to overwhelm me, making panic rear its ugly head in my chest.

I knocked lightly on the door to the office Raiden disappeared into, to find him looking through a folder on his desk.

"Hey," he said, frowning at the sheets of paper.

"What's that?"

"This?" He glanced at me. "Just some family stuff I left here. A few years back, I was working on trying to get more information on my mother's family. After she was married off, she pretty much stayed in Xanan. I only remember my grandparents visiting a handful of times."

I stepped further into the room and moved to his side and peered down at the papers.

"It's not much," I murmured.

"I know." He sighed. "Mother liked to keep her life so private. I guess I never realized how much until lately. I never questioned it as a kid. I just knew I loved her and she loved me. Now I wonder, you know?" He shuffled through the small stack.

"Do you know your grandparents' names?"

"Theodore and Isabella," he said, pushing an old photo at me. I picked it up and studied the couple in it. They looked like nice, ordinary people. He wore glasses. She had a big smile with blonde hair.

"Are they still alive?"

He shrugged. "I honestly don't know. They didn't come around enough for me to notice their absence. I think my mother preferred it that way. Arranged marriages aren't always a treat for the whole family."

I watched as he shuffled through more papers. The desire to take his sadness away overcame me.

"I love you," I said softly.

He paused his work to look up at me. A tiny smile flitted across his lips. "I love you too, Everly."

"Is it true what Damien said? About you, um, wanting to have sex in public?"

He let out a soft laugh. "He's an ass. I got drunk one night and said that. He hasn't forgotten it."

"But is it true?"

His lips twitched at the corners, the smile threatening to spill onto his lips. "Yes. I've spent my life hidden in the shadows. I always wondered what that would be like to experience. Taking the woman I love and making love to her, the threat of being caught real." He took my hand and pulled onto his lap and kissed along my jaw. "Bending you over the balcony in my bedroom that overlooks my kingdom has been weighing heavily on my mind."

Goosebumps swept over my skin at his words.

"Yeah?" I breathed out.

"Yes. I want to claim you there someday."

"I think I'd like that."

"Me too." He turned my face to his and pressed his lips to mine. "How did I get so lucky to get a woman like you?"

"Fate," I said, nipping his bottom lip.

"I'll send them a thank you card."

"Hey, sorry to interrupt," Eric called out, sounding awkward as he stood in the doorway. I broke away from Raiden, my face heating.

Raiden didn't seem fazed in the slight and raised his brows at Eric, waiting for him to continue.

"Damien wants to talk. I think he's getting antsy."

Raiden laughed and brought me to my feet. He stuffed the papers back into his drawer and grabbed a set of keys from it before taking my hand and following Eric out of the office.

Raiden flicked his wrist, and the purple shimmer faded away.

"About damn time," Damien grumbled. "I thought I was going to have to wait until I got back to the house to have Sloane undo that shit for me."

"The silence was nice," I said with a laugh.

Damien grinned. "Don't get used to it. I plan on making up for lost time."

"Great." Raiden shook his head. "You can do it in the car, though. We should get going."

"Why are we taking a car, anyway?" Damien asked. "Why don't we just meld there?"

"Ever is still learning and hitching a ride is uncomfortable for her," Raiden said, leading the way out of the house. "If we need to leave the car and meld back, fine. I just don't want to be using energy we might need."

"Makes sense," Eric said as we stepped into the garage to find a blacked out sedan waiting for us.

Raiden open the front passenger door for me, and I slid onto the cool leather. Damien and Eric got into the back and Raiden moved to the driver's spot. The garbage door opened behind us and he breathed out.

"Ready?" he asked, glancing over at me with worry in his eyes.

"Ready," I said. I moved my hand to rest on his thigh. He gave me a grateful smile before putting the car into reverse and backing out.

Ready was all I could be. I knew how important this trip was to Raiden. It wasn't just to him though. We would be one step closer to the next part of our story.

RAIDEN

"Stay by my side," I instructed Ever as we got out of the car in Ravenvale Grove an hour later. I'd parked the car on the edge of a cobblestone street before entering the town. I knew our world well enough to understand cars and things of that nature weren't always welcome within communities. Since I wasn't familiar with this place, I opted to not draw a lot of attention to ourselves.

"It looks nice. It's big," Damien commented as he looked around. "Your mom grew up here?"

"Yeah." I took in the scenery. As far as places went, this one seemed serene. There wasn't a lot of bustle, but it was early in the morning.

Small buildings were nestled along the edge of the city, with the sizes increasing the deeper into the city one went. Snow still glistened on the ground, but it wasn't as deep as it was at Dementon. The cobblestone streets were empty, making our walk easier.

"Do you know where the family crypt is?" Eric asked as he looked around.

"I'm assuming it's at the cemetery. I only saw one on the map," I said as we walked. Ever's green eyes darted around as she took everything in. I knew she was probably nervous about an attack. I reached out and took her hand.

Her focus snapped to me.

"No worries, love. You're safe." I said into her mind.

"Anything can happen."

"It can, but I promise it won't. At least not right now."

"Why don't we just meld?" she asked.

"We can if it'll make you feel better."

She nodded, and I pulled out of her mind.

"Let's meld. We can skip through the shadows faster, and it'll put Ever at ease," I said. "It's good practice at such a short distance."

"I was wondering if we were going to do that," Damien said. "I was just about to suggest it. Can't ever be too careful."

He was right. We shimmered and began the leap through the shadows, my hand wrapped firmly around Ever's. I took the lead, having memorized the map the night before.

By the time we reached the cemetery, the sun was higher in the sky. We skidded to a halt in the center of the old stone garden and looked around.

"Damn, this place probably has Specials from half a millennium ago." Eric peered around at the massive graveyard with its old, cracked stones.

"I hate cemeteries." Ever shivered as she clutched my hand tighter.

"You hate cemeteries?" Damien grinned over at her. "Damn. And here I thought they were your favorite place to adventure."

She rolled her eyes at him. "Definitely not."

"Come on." I tugged her hand. "Let's split up. Eric, take the west side. Damien, take the east. Ever and I will go north. Keep in contact. You know the drill"."

Our group split, Eric and Damien darting off in opposite directions as we moved forward.

"What do you think we'll find?" Ever asked as we walked through the cracked stones.

"I don't know. Hopefully, some answers, but I'm not holding my breath. In my experience, when you go searching for answers, you usually come back with more questions."

"Ain't that the truth," she muttered.

We were quiet as we walked. I breathed in deeply, enjoying the fresh air. The small bit of snow on the ground crunched beneath our feet.

"Do we have a plan on what we'll do once we find the crypt?" she asked.

I swallowed. "I want to check it."

"You mean open it?" She visibly shuddered.

"I have to know. If my brother is in his tomb, I'll accept it."

"And if he's not?" Ever looked at me with those pretty green eyes of hers. I could see the concern clouding in their jade depths. "Then what?"

"I don't know," I answered honestly. What would I do? Where would I look? My father said my brother was laid to rest here. From what I'd gathered, he hadn't made much of an effort to visit the place, and why would he? He already said he focused on what he had, not on what he'd lost.

"I'm scared," she said after a beat of silence.

"Why?"

"I'm afraid of what you aren't going to find." Her words were ominous and made me swallow hard. In all honesty, I was afraid too.

"I have a request," I said softly.

She looked to me.

I licked my lips, hating the next words that would tumble out of my mouth. "If my brother is in his crypt, I need you to wake him."

"What?" She stopped in her tracks, her hand falling away from mine.

I stopped and turned back to her. "Everly, the prediction is a breadcrumb. It said to find him—"

"Yeah. *Find* him. It didn't say shit about me bringing a dead baby back to life!" She blanched at her words. "I-I can't do that."

I approached her and captured her lips against mine. She melted into me like she always did, the tension leaving her body.

"I need this," I whispered against her soft lips. "Please."

"What good will it do? He's just an infant," she whispered in a thick voice. "He has no memories."

85

"All things have memories," I said gently. "Even the smallest things. *Please.*"

She winced as she took me in. "Raiden... it's a baby. A child. I-I don't know if I can even look at it let alone bring it back. And say I can bring it back. What the hell are we going to do with a zombie baby?"

"You'll put him back to sleep," I murmured.

"So I have to bring it back and then send it off?" She shook her head at me. "Do you realize what you're asking of me? What if I can't do it? What if I can bring him back and then can't get him to go away? Then what?"

"Then I'll figure something out. If there are answers in that crypt, we have to get them. I don't care how many of the dead we have to wake. Our job is to save our world. And so we will."

She sighed. "Just so you know, I am the least excited I've ever been. Un-excited. Like, I'd rather take a nap on one of these graves than do what you're asking of me."

"I know," I said gently, brushing her dark hair away from her face. "I'm sorry. You know I wouldn't ask it of you if there were another way. Besides, we don't know what we'll find once we get there."

"That's what I'm afraid of," she said in a soft voice.

I backed away and took her hand in mine and led her forward.

It was what I was afraid of too.

EVERLY

I dreaded the moment we'd find Raiden's family crypt. While I knew him asking me to bring his twin back to the land of the living was a huge possibility, it still made me cringe thinking about it.

My necromancing with Basil Hessen hadn't exactly been a lot of fun. I shuddered to think what bringing an infant back would be like. The thought made bile rise in my throat.

I left Raiden alone with his thoughts as we walked through the cemetery. It was a half hour into our journey through the massive graveyard before he gripped my hand tighter.

"What's wrong?"

"I don't know," he murmured, rubbing his chest and frowning.

I looked around, only to see the place was empty.

"I-I think we need to go this way." He tugged my hand and led me to the right. I stumbled along behind him as he swept quickly through the stones, his pace picking up the further we went.

"Damnit, Raiden," I hissed at him as I tripped over a smaller stone and nearly ate shit. My words didn't have an affect on him. He released my hand and ran forward through a thicket of dark trees.

I swore and took off after him, my shin throbbing from where I'd crashed against the headstone.

I skidded to a halt as I entered the thicket to find him staring up at a dark mausoleum.

"How did you know?" I breathed out, coming to his side.

"It was a pull," he murmured. "I felt it."

He stepped forward and pressed his hand to the door. A blue glow surrounded it for a moment before it cracked open. He glanced back at me, his aquamarine eyes flashing with a look I couldn't quite place.

"You can wait here," he murmured. "If you're afraid."

I steeled myself. "I'm coming with you." He gave me a smile after I reached out and took his hand. Quickly, I sent out a message in my mind to Eric and Damien with our location and followed Raiden into the dark crypt, a blue flame in his hand for light.

Expecting a simple room with a coffin in the center of it was stupid of me. We did enter a room. However, it was empty. A stairway led deeper beneath the crypt. I licked my lips, really hating cemeteries, even if we were in a place with Raiden's family.

"Come on," he murmured, moving to the stairs. I followed him as he descended, my nerves getting the better of me. When we reached the bottom, he moved forward, his blue light casting a dull glow around us. Dark outlines of coffins signaled we were definitely in the right place.

"Shadow," I called out nervously when his hand slipped from mine.

"It's OK," he said. "Everyone in here is already dead."

"That's what I'm afraid of." I moved to his dim glow and focused everything I had on making my own light. The static in me grew. Instinct drove me and I flung my hands out. The room ignited in a burst of color, the torches on the walls glowing with crackling orange flames.

Raiden paused and took in the now bright room before he looked back at me.

"You never cease to amaze me," he said.

"I don't like the dark," I offered with a shrug.

His eyes flashed with his sadness for me. I hated when he wore that look. I shoved a smile onto my face, hoping it would make him lose that damn expression.

He turned away from me and continued through the maze of coffins.

"You guys are deep in this bitch," Damien said as he and Eric came down the stairs. "I can't believe how massive this cemetery is."

"It's too big," I muttered.

"Find anything?" Eric asked as he stopped beside me. Damien tugged a strand of my hair as he passed by to get to Raiden.

"Nothing. Raiden felt a pull to come here though," I said.

Eric nodded. "I guess that makes sense. All of us have been having these déjà vu type things lately. Amanda told me she knew the answers to her astronomy quiz last week and didn't know how she knew. Jared said he felt like he'd done something before, only to have to do it later. Plus, Raiden's mom was incredibly psychic. Coupled with you, I can imagine he's just sorting through a lot of new abilities."

It made sense, as frightening as that was.

"Come on. Let's find his brother and get out of here," I said, moving forward. Eric followed me, both of us scanning the names engraved on the plaques in front of the coffins.

"You're more tense than usual," Eric commented. "He wants you to raise him, doesn't he?"

I nodded tightly, glancing over to where Raiden was frowning down at a coffin. He turned and looked at another as Damien moved away from the one he was standing at.

"You're not alone." Eric reached out and gave my hand a squeeze. "Today. Tomorrow. Whenever. It's OK to be scared, but it's also OK to let others help you."

"I don't think you can help me with this." I grimaced, my body trembling slightly as the wild idea of having to possibly bring an infant back to life took hold.

"Trust me. We can. We'll be by your side. You won't be alone. Promise." He gave me a gentle smile that made me breathe out, my anxiety washing away. He was right. I knew they'd be at my side. They were three of the most powerful Specials in our world.

I was a fourth.

I'd be OK.

"Here," Raiden shouted.

I broke away from Eric and rushed to him, stopping at his side moments later. I stared down at the plaque that read Kazimir Wesley Hawthorne with Damien and Eric now beside us.

"This is him," Raiden whispered, his voice shaking. "My brother."

Damien clapped him on the shoulder as I squeezed his hand. The coffin was smaller than the others and gold with ornate gems stuck into the side. Rubies. I swallowed and looked to Raiden. His eyes wavered as he stared down at it.

"Do we have a plan?" Eric asked softly.

Raiden visibly swallowed and was quiet for a moment before he looked at me with wide, pleading eyes.

Shit.

"Everly, I—"

"I'll do it," I whispered. "For you, I'll do it."

The tension melted away from his body. He drew me in and pressed his lips to mine in a tender kiss.

"Thank you," he whispered when he pulled away.

I nodded tightly, my anxiety kicking in.

"So we're just going to, um, open it?" Damien asked.

Raiden nodded wordlessly.

"Are you sure you want to do that?" Eric glanced between me and Raiden. "I mean, it's your brother, Raiden. Is this how you want to see him?"

Raiden stared down at the coffin for a moment before he answered. "I have to know. I'm meant to know." He reached forward and waved his hand over the coffin. The seal cracked, and the top creaked open.

I held my breath as I stared into the empty space.

"Where is he?" Raiden called out dumbly.

"Well, shit," Damien muttered.

Eric said nothing, opting to stare into the space with me. There was no baby. No brother. It was simply... empty.

"Wait," Eric said after a moment. He frowned and reached into the coffin. Nestled beneath the white satin pillow was an envelope. He pulled it out and handed it to Raiden.

"It has my name on it," Raiden murmured as he looked down at it.

We watched silently as he opened the letter and pulled it out. His eyes scanned it quickly, a muscle thrumming along his jaw.

"What is it?" Damien asked.

Raiden slammed the coffin closed and shoved the letter into Damien's chest and stormed away.

"Let him be," Eric said, grabbing my hand to stop me from following him. "He needs a minute."

I watched Raiden disappear up the stairs, the door slamming closed behind him as he left.

"This is weird. What does it mean?" Damien held the letter out to Eric and I to read.

Only one sentence was on the worn parchment.

Follow the red.

I froze as I stared down at the script.

"What the hell does follow the red mean?" Eric murmured, his brows crinkled as he read the sentence.

I breathed out.

I knew what it meant. Dyre. Follow Dyre.

Follow me.

RAIDEN

A week passed since we were in Ravenvale Grove. One long week of me rolling everything over in my head on repeat. My brother's body was missing. No answers. More questions. Where is he? Why would someone take his body? Was there ever even a body? What did follow the red mean?

And the worst one of all. What if he's still alive? Does he know I'm his brother? Is he looking for me too?

I planned on asking my father about it, but decided against it. If he didn't know, then it was probably for the best. I had no answers for him if he asked. Maybe once I found out the answers, I could go to him about it.

The problem with getting the answers was that I had nothing to go on. My mother was dead. No one knew of his existence to start with. It was a lot of dead ends that frustrated the shit out of me.

I rubbed my eyes before going back to the book I was reading on the Old Words. There had to be something there. So far, nothing that I'd looked up pointed in any direction of follow the red. There was one thing that was bothering me. It had to do with what I'd seen in a vision. A vision I had not that long ago. One that made my guts churn.

I hated thinking about the image in my head. In fact, I've been trying to shove it out of my mind since I'd seen it. The vision was one of Everly surrounded in flames, screaming my name. I'd seen the red cloaks. While I didn't want it to be what I needed to follow, I also didn't have another explanation for what the letter meant.

Ever had been exceptionally quiet the last few days. I didn't know if it was because of how quiet I'd been and she was simply giving me space, or if something was genuinely bothering her. When I'd asked her, she'd given me a smile and answered by kissing me.

I flipped the pages in the book until I reached the end. Nothing stuck out at me, so I close the book and let out a breath. I sat with my head in my hands as the minutes ticked by, not sure what I was going to do. At this point, it seemed like a losing battle. There just weren't any answers.

A knock on my door had me lifting my head to see Ever standing in the doorway, her black robes hanging loosely from her body and dark circles rimming her eyes.

Immediately, I got to my feet and went to her.

"What's wrong?" I tilted her chin up so she was looking at me.

"I need to talk to you," she said, peering up at me with green, glistening eyes.

I took her by the hand and led her to my couch and pulled her onto the seat beside me. I shifted sideways so I could look at her.

"Talk to me."

She visibly swallowed. "I've been thinking about your brother. I-I think he's still alive."

"I do too," I admitted softly. It was the only logical answer to everything. "But I have run out of leads. I don't know what to do at this point."

She licked her lips before she went still. The only thing moving were her hands as she fidgeted with them nervously in her lap. I waited for her to say something, watching as her legs began to bounce nervously.

"Everly, sweetheart. Just tell me."

"It isn't like I don't want to tell you. It's more like… I can't.

I frowned. "Why can't you tell me? What's going on?"

"That's the thing. If I tell you, I don't want to hurt you. Like last time." She looked at me from beneath a fringe of dark hair, guilt marring her pretty face.

I reached for her hand and took in mine before giving it a squeeze. "I said I would follow you. I meant it. But you also know that I need more information. How can I follow if I don't have all the information?"

"Raiden, I would never do anything to jeopardize you or our relationship. Not intentionally."

I knew she was talking about Blackburn and everything that went down with him over the last few weeks.

"I know you wouldn't. What am I missing, Ever?"

"That I want to tell you, but I'm just unable to." Her eyes widened as she stared at me. I watched as her leg jumped, her nerves clearly getting the better of her.

"You're cursed?"

Again she remained silent, but her eyes were wide and her leg jumped again as she twisted her fingers in her lap.

"Okay," I said, letting out a deep breath. "You need to understand something. I can't help you unless I know what's going on. This entire *can't tell me* situation feels like something I should have the information to." I raise my eyebrows at her. "You see where I'm coming from, right? It seems dangerous to not be able to tell someone something important, you know?"

She nodded and twisted her fingers more in her lap. Her breathing picked up, signaling she would probably have a panic attack within minutes. I reached for her hand and gave it a squeeze.

"Everly," I whispered. "I love you. I know how curses work. I know you can't say anything to me to give it away. At least in so many words. I am going to assume that is the situation. I thought it since it happened. But if this is something that's going to save the world, it shouldn't be kept a secret. You know how dangerous it is for secrets."

"I know how dangerous. Secrets can destroy everything. I only need you to trust me."

"I do trust you. It's him I don't trust. Blackburn. Thinking he wants to keep it a secret unnerves me."

"Follow the red." She breathed in deeply. "I am the red, Shadow. Me. You have to follow me."

I released her hand and ran my fingers through my hair, frustration eating at me. There wasn't any winning. I trusted her with my life, but I wouldn't trust him with it. Something didn't seem right, and I refused to blindly join whatever the hell was going on. It didn't matter if it were Ever. I had a duty to my people first and foremost, even if I loved her. Once I had all the information I needed on Blackburn, I would make my decision. We were in a precarious situation, one where there wasn't a simple answer. To blindly walk into something that could end our world seemed like a bad idea.

" I'd like to make a deal." I looked over at her and didn't wait for her to respond before I continued. "I will follow you. Wherever. If something comes up and proves this is a very bad idea, you have to promise to abandon it and follow me instead. Deal?"

She nodded thoughtfully, her legs slowing their bounce until she became still. "I agree."

"Good." I let out a sigh of relief. "Can you tell me about the red now?"

"Maybe," she said, biting her bottom lip. "Because I can't tell you everything, I will tell you what I can. You need to also understand that I want more than anything to tell you everything, but I can't until you are fully in. You need to be at my side. For real. Forever."

She paused before continuing. "I'd feel better if you had a weapon. You know, in case something happens."

I cringed at the idea of harming her. It hadn't been easy to when she'd attacked me after the curse took hold of her. It sickened me to cause her harm and subdue her.

"Trust me, I'll be fine," I said, giving her a reassuring smile.

She grimaced but seemed to accept it. "You wear black. Do you know what color Cipher wear?"

I crinkled my brows as I considered her words. "Not really. I see them in black mostly."

"Never red?"

"Red sticks out too much. They try to blend in so they don't get caught. They wear street clothes even sometimes. Just like Natties."

"So Cipher doesn't wear red," she whispered. "I-I wear red."

"When do you wear red?" I asked, holding my breath.

"When I-I'm. . . " her words faltered. A look of panic swept over her face. "I can't say."

I nodded. "It's OK, sweetheart. I understand. Don't push it."

"I'm sorry. I-I just need you to trust me," her voice faltered and her eyes glazed over. Immediately, I reached for her as she swayed. I knew that look. She was going to rattle off something that would chill me to my core.

"The fire will burn
The tides will turn
Shadow recedes into darkness
All is lost when he grows heartless
A new king crowned through the flame
And only one holds the blame
When he draws his last breath
And she shall be called Death
She will pass from this life to the next
A new prince at her side
A brother. A lover. The second. The other.
All is lost if they cannot align
Three souls must combine
The hour is five
And she will die
The world will tumble
As the old crown crumbles"

Her eyes had grown to stark white. Her breath shuddered out as the tension left her trembling body. I dragged her to me, my pulse roaring in my ears as her words repeated inside my head.

"You're going to lose me," she sobbed softly. "I-I saw it. I remember it. I-I die. You won't be able to save me, Raiden. Shadow. I'm going to die."

"I won't let you, baby. I promise it. I swear it," I choked out, my heart in my throat. There was no way in hell I was going to lose the most important thing in my life. I couldn't handle it if I did. The thought alone made me so heartsick I thought I'd vomit.

I clung to her tighter as she sniffled into my chest. She was now on my lap, her fingers twisted into my black button down, her tears warm and wet against me.

"Baby, please," I choked out. "No. Don't. I swear it. I will blood oath it if I must. I'm not letting you go. No one is going to touch you in any way. You belong to me. You always will. Nothing." I forced her face off my chest so I could thumb away her tears. "Nothing is going to change that. Do you understand me? Nothing, Everly." I kissed her soft, tear soaked lips, that ugly ache in my throat that had been clawing at me for weeks taking hold. I shoved it down like I always did as I deepened our wet, salty kiss.

"Mine. My girl. My queen. My Mancer," I said, kissing her feverishly.

She whimpered against my lips at every kiss until she was parting her lips to glide her tongue along mine.

An electric buzz ebbed through my body like a low pulsing wave, the ache growing stronger in my throat.

I need to taste her. I need her to be part of me.

She cried out as I bit her bottom lip, drawing her blood into my mouth in the smallest of droplets. The ache grew intense as her sweet taste teased my tongue.

"Ah, Raiden," she called out as I released her lip, only to move to her neck where I sucked against her pulse point, knowing damn well I was leaving my mark and promising myself I wasn't going to heal it either. I wanted everyone to know she was mine. I'd paint her body in my kisses if it would prove to the world who she belonged to.

"Tell me yes," I growled, nipping at her skin. *Please tell me no.* What's happening to me? What am I asking of her?

"Y-Yes. Please."

The urge to sink my teeth into her soft flesh overwhelmed me as her words tumbled from her mouth. My head spun. Sweat dotted my forehead as I ripped her shirt open, sending her buttons scattering across my office and displaying her glorious breasts in her black lace bra.

I shoved her straps off her shoulders as I fought the urge to bite her. The urge was stronger than my fear of what was happening to me, and that was saying something.

Where I was usually gentle with her, I wasn't this time. My touch was rough and demanding as I fisted her soft black hair, letting my fingers tangle in it. I forced her head to the side and ran my teeth along her neck, my body trembling as I struggled to fight the ache that was steadily growing stronger in my soul.

No. No. NO! Don't. Stop. What the hell am I doing? I can't. Gods help me, I can't. . .

A cry left her lips as the ache won. I bit into her neck, sinking my teeth deep into her flesh. She jerked, her hands on my chest as she tried to shove me away, but I couldn't. I wouldn't release her. Whatever was happening to me was taking over.

I growled as her blood flowed freely into my mouth. Each swallow made my eyes roll back in my head from the deliciousness of my Everly that ebbed into my veins. All reason left my mind as I drank from her.

Even her cries of pain didn't stop me.

I shoved her onto her back, my teeth still buried deep, and pushed her skirt up.

With her chest heaving and her fingers twisted in my shirt, I hauled my pants down as fast as I could and pushed into her tight heat as she cried out louder. Her body jerked against mine with each deep thrust.

And I continued to drink from her.

Her cries grew quieter until her hands fell away from me and her body grew limp. Her heart thudded unevenly beneath my body as I found my release inside her.

Her blood flowed slower. Less. Her heart stuttered. Her breathing slowed.

The haze I'd been under left me. I pulled away from her and stared down in horror at what I'd done. Her creamy skin was smeared with blood and damp with sweat. Where she usually had a beautiful flush, it was now pale white, the pretty rose color gone.

"No. No," I whispered in a choked voice, the taste of her still on my tongue. Immediately, I pressed my hands to her chest and forced everything I had into healing her. Her heart thudded faster. Harder. Her eyelids fluttered open.

"Everly," I rasped, cradling her face in my hands. "Baby."

She stared up at me through bleary eyes. "You bit me," she whispered, her voice cracking.

"I-I did. I'm sorry," I choked out. Shit. What the actual hell. . .

"You were going to kill me," she said, her voice cracking. "I was scared. It-It hurt so much." A soft sob left her trembling lips.

I couldn't bear it. I pressed my forehead to hers.

"I'm sorry. I-I don't know what happened. I'm so sorry. Please," I sobbed, my tears dropping onto her bloody cheeks. Gods, I'd made a mess. "I'll fix this. I promise. I'll fix it."

I pressed my palm to her forehead and forced her unconscious. She went limp once more, and I reached out to Eric in my mind after tucking myself away.

"I need you in my office. Just you. Hurry."

Eric stirred in my mind, and I felt him moving toward me. Moments later, he appeared in a black flurry of shadow, his blue eyes wide. His gaze shot from me to Ever before his eyes widened, and he rushed forward and dropped to his knees beside her.

"What the hell happened?" He demanded, pushing her tangled hair away from her face. I hadn't had time to cover her properly. Eric could see her in her bra, but at least her skirt and panties were back in place.

"Why are you both covered in blood?"

"I-I need you to go into her head. I need you to sift through her memories. I-I need you to make her forget."

"What?" He crinkled his brows as he took me in. "What the hell is going on?"

"Just do it," I whispered. "Change the memory. Please."

Eric studied me for a moment before he turned away to face Ever, a muscle popping along his jaw. With shaking hands, he reached for her and cradled her head in his hands and closed his eyes. The familiar white glow that came with his sifting surrounded them as he worked through her mind.

His facial features changed a few times before he released her and sat back on his heels, his face flushed and sweaty from the effort.

"Clean her up," he said in a thick voice as he got to his feet.

"Did you fix it?"

He snorted as he stared down at her. "I did what I could."

I stared at Ever's sleeping form and didn't look at Eric when I spoke. "You saw what I did."

"I did," he answered.

"I-I'm not a monster. I don't know what's happening to me." I wiped at my eyes before the tears trickled out. "I've never done anything like this before. I'm afraid." I finally dragged my gaze from my sleeping Mancer to my best friend. "What's happening to me?"

The anger slipped from his face. "I don't know, man. I-I've never seen anything like it. I've never heard of anything like it. You're a vampire—"

"I'm not," I snarled, venom in my words. "I've never been bitten. I'm born of shifter and fae blood. You know that—"

"What I know is you drank from her until you nearly killed her. What I know is she's half-naked, covered in blood, and you want me to change her memories."

I said nothing, the guilt eating at me as I studied her. I was afraid of losing her. I'd just promised I'd keep her safe and then this shit? I tightened my hands into fists.

"I need to get her cleaned up and into bed," I said.

"You need to figure out what the hell is going on."

I nodded tightly. "Yeah. That too."

"Raiden. I'm serious. Something insane is happening. We can't have you going around biting innocent people and nearly murdering—"

I was on my feet in a flash and shoving him against the wall, my fists twisted in his uniform.

"She is my life. You know she is. Whatever happened wasn't me. It wasn't me. You know I'd never hurt her—"

"But you did," he said, staring right back at me.

I released him and took a step back. "What do I do?"

"I think you need to leave," he answered solemnly. "Get your head sorted. I'll keep watch over her. We all will. We have the Arcane Ball coming up. You need to have your shit together so you can go because it's not exactly something the future king of our world can miss. I'll handle everything here. We need you, Raiden. She needs you. Whatever the hell just happened can't happen again. Get her cleaned up. I'll go with you. I hope you understand why I can't leave you alone."

I nodded tightly and went to her. I scooped her into my arms and melded to her bedroom, Eric following me.

"I'll wait right here," he said as I laid her on her bed.

I said nothing and went to her bathroom and ran warm water onto a washcloth before returning to her. I made fast work of cleaning every bit of her I'd touched as Eric stood with his back to me. Once I had her cleared of blood, I changed her into her pajama shorts and t-shirt before tucking her into bed. I pushed more healing into her and listened as she let out a contented sigh in her sleep.

"I love you," I whispered, clasping her hand in mine. "I messed up. Something isn't right. I'll fix it though. I'll figure it out. I promise. Just. . . listen to Eric while I'm gone. Be safe. Please be safe, Everly. I'll come if I need to, but I need you to try for me. Stay away from Blackburn. Maybe this is just stress or something. . ." my voice trailed off. I pressed a gentle kiss to her lips after a moment of self-loathing. "I'll see you soon, my love."

I released her hand and moved away from her.

"Take care of her. You're in charge. She's everything to me, Eric."

"I know she is," he said, glancing over his shoulder at her. "She means a lot to all of us. Do whatever you need to do to get back here. I'll make sure she's OK."

"Thank you, brother," I said. I melded into my shadow form and cast one last look at Ever before I left her room to go to mine, my guts churning.

The moment I was in my bathroom, I vomited the contents of my guts into the toilet and sobbed like a baby. I was sure Eric could hear everything, but to hell with it. Maybe I'd been cursed. That was the only explanation I had as to why I was chewing on my fiancée and nearly killing her.

I hated myself. My promise meant nothing when that damn ache came. And I'd acted on it like some sort of monster.

Shoving myself to my feet, I went to my sink and rinsed my mouth out and cleaned the blood off me before going to my closet and grabbing an overnight bag. I stuffed a few things into it before taking my shadow form.

Before the pull to go to my girl and crawl into bed and hold her grew too strong, I slipped away into the shadows, desperate to figure out what the hell was going on.

EVERLY

I hadn't heard from Raiden in a week. I'd woken up with a
hell of a headache and the memory of having a vision and
nothing else. Complete blackness. Eric said I'd fallen and hit my head.
Raiden healed me and had to go do some super secret Order thing
and was too far away to contact any of us.

Being without him was lonely. I missed him like crazy. Having
Eric in charge was a lot different from when Raiden was in charge.
Eric was looser on things. Instead of assigning people to things, he
asked for volunteers. He brought me sweets from a shop in Xanan and
we'd ate them together as we watched a movie in my bedroom after
training.

He called everyone into the living room for a meeting as I walked
back from classes. Thinking maybe Raiden was back, I zipped back to
the Conexus house as fast as I could, only to see Raiden's seat empty.
My heart sank as I settled onto the couch next to Mason.

"Word on Shadow?" Jared called out as he reached for a sandwich I
assumed Sloane made.

"Nothing," Eric said, his gaze darting to me quickly. "Shouldn't be
long now. He needs to return before the Arcane Ball next week. It's
mandatory he attends."

I still didn't have a dress for that. A ball at a palace where my fiancé was going to be the king? Yeah, pretty sure my high-low dress wouldn't cut it.

"Are we sure he's OK?" I called out. I asked Eric that every damn time I saw him.

He gave me the same sad look he'd given me each time I'd ask. "I'm sure he's fine. If he weren't, we'd know."

I nodded glumly like I always did.

"You can't feel him? Even at whatever distance he's at?" Brandon asked.

I shook my head. "Not really. I feel. . .empty in a way. I can feel we're connected, but that's it. It's like a heavy tug on my heart."

Amara scoffed from her corner. I ignored it.

"He's had to go off like this before," Adam said, offering me a sympathetic look. "Longest was. . .what? A month last time?"

Chloe nodded. "Just a few days over, actually."

"It won't be that long this time," Eric said.

"How do you know? Did he even tell you where he was going or what he was doing?" Amara demanded.

"I have a decent idea," Eric shot back. "So chill. He'll be back."

Amara rolled her eyes and crossed her arms over her chest.

"Tonight I wanted to call this meeting to get volunteers for a fairly easy nest sweep of some carrion. It really shouldn't take long. Jared did some recon, and based on the info we've gotten from the Order, there is only a handful in the nest."

"I'll go," Mason said. "I need more practice, anyway."

"That's one," Eric said, nodding in his direction. "Damien?"

Damien had been quiet the entire time, something totally abnormal for him. I glanced over to see him staring at me. When he noticed I'd caught him, he offered me a crooked smile that didn't quite reach his eyes.

"I'll go," he said. "If Sloane goes."

"Why do you always drag me into your messes, Wick? I'd like a day off for once," she grumbled.

"Why can't you go?" Amara called out to Eric. "Why can't Ever?

You didn't even bother to send her on a simple recon mission and she hasn't had to do patrols all week—"

Eric held his hand up to silence her. "In the absence of our General, it's imperative that Ever remain in the safety of Conexus house. I've given my word to Raiden that I won't leave her side. We remain here where she's safest. None of us have power like Raiden does to protect her. If something happens to her, she's screwed."

"Good," Amara muttered.

I shook my head and looked down at my hands. "I'll do patrols tonight. Chloe, Amanda, and Sloane have been pulling double duty for me. It's not fair. I can do it. I really don't mind."

"No—" Eric started.

"I'm doing it," I cut in. "I'm going crazy just sitting here. I need to get out and do something, even if it is patrols."

Eric sighed. "Fine. Girls and Adam, you have the night off. Ever and I will do patrols."

The girls whooped and Adam planted a kiss on Chloe's lips. I smiled at them, grateful I could do something. I didn't like Raiden playing favorites or whatever him and Eric had concocted. I'd much rather pull my weight.

"I'll go on the nest shit," Jared said. "If Damien goes and lets Sloane have a night off."

Damien groaned. "Fine. Don't say I never gave you anything." He gave Sloane a pointed look. She smiled back at him.

"One more." Eric glanced around. "Amara?"

"No thanks," she said, looking at her nails. "If Ever doesn't have to do anything, then neither do I. I mean, what do I need to do, Lieutenant? Get on my knees for you like she does when Raiden isn't around?"

I glared at her as I sat forward. Mason held his arm out and blocked me from getting to my feet. He raised a brow at me to let me know he'd restrain me if he had to.

"OK. Well, I was going to be nice, but since you're provoking me, Amara, you're going to the carrion nest and you'll be pulling doubles for patrol the rest of the week, starting when you get home.

Have a great time." Eric's stare at her was even, no emotion on his face.

She let out an angry snarl and stormed from the room.

"You don't really get on your knees for Eric when Gen's gone, do you?" Damien called out, his teasing grin back in place.

I gave him the finger, to which he burst into a peel of laughter before Eric dismissed everyone. Conexus dispersed, leaving me alone with Eric.

"Have you gotten a dress yet?" he asked.

"You know I haven't. I can't even leave this place. Hell, I don't want to leave. You know that."

He flopped down beside me. "I know. Guess I was just trying to make conversation."

"Is he really on a mission? It just seems so unlike him to disappear like this without trying to reach out to me."

"He can feel you, Ever. You know that. He knows you're safe. He's focusing right now."

I hated he made sense.

"I'm going to nap then before we go out on patrols."

"OK." He watched as I got to my feet. "You know, if you don't want to do patrols, I can just assign someone—"

"I'm doing the patrol. It's not fair that I don't."

He nodded. "Fine. See you in few hours. Sleep well."

I waved him off and darted to Raiden's room. I'd taken to sleeping in there in his absence. I guess it made me feel close to him while he was gone. I flopped onto his bed and closed my eyes before reaching out with my mind in the hopes I could talk to him. When I was met with a blank wall, I whispered my words into his room instead.

"Come back to me soon, Shadow."

WE'D BEEN PATROLLING for the last hour. The grounds were quiet, like always. Now and then we'd see a straggler getting back to their dorms after god knew what adventure they'd been on.

"How are the dreams you were having?" Eric asked as we walked down the cobblestone path between the science building and astronomy tower.

"Fine. I've learned to stop myself from entering the veil when I sense them coming on. I usually wake myself up or forced another dream into my head."

"Lucid dreaming?"

I shrugged. "I guess. Whatever it is, I'm getting better at it."

"I'm glad. You had us worried there for a while."

I didn't say anything else as we walked. Truth be told, I'd been worried. Getting chased by rakes wasn't just a damn dream. It was a total nightmare.

Eric cleared his throat. "I, uh, know what your prediction was."

I gave him the side-eye. "You do? Same as last time? You got to see it with me?"

"Not really. But yeah."

"You don't make sense."

He sighed. "I know. I'm sorry. I saw it in your head when you, um, fell."

"Sorry," I said awkwardly, not really sure what I was apologizing for. It wasn't like I could help it.

We were quiet for a long time before two shadowy figures appeared on the path ahead of us.

"Great," Eric grunted. "I hate when students are out past curfew. It's always a mess having to deal with them."

I said nothing as I realized who the two were.

Nev and Marcus.

Eric must have realized it too, because he swore under his breath as we approached them.

"It's past curfew," Eric said. "But I'm sure you guys know it."

"We do," Nev said, his gaze sliding over to me. "We were actually looking for Ever."

"What for?" I asked, ignoring the way Eric fidgeted beside me.

"It's been a long time. I'd say that's no way to treat me," Nev said easily. "With our history and all."

My face heated at his words. "Nev," I murmured. "Stop."

"Eric, would you mind terribly if we borrowed Ever for just a moment?" Marcus asked. "We'll just be right over there." He pointed to a small cluster of trees. "You can wait for her if you want or we can return her to Conexus house when we're done."

"Not happening. It's past curfew. You need to get back to your dorms before you get written up," Eric said. "Conexus doesn't associate outside our ranks."

"Oh, come now, Craft. How about you let Ever decide what she wants to do?" Nev cocked his head at Eric. "Taking away too many freedoms can push anyone into the arms of the wicked."

"Yeah, I know," Eric snapped at him. "Which is why I'm keeping her from you."

"Me?" Nev let out a laugh. "You must be hanging out with Hawthorne too much. You know, him and I get along rather well when he isn't being a dick."

Before Eric could say anything, I spoke. "I do actually need to talk to you guys. Maybe we can meet tomorrow night? And Eric can come?"

I knew I made a promise to Raiden to stay away from Nev, but both he and Marcus were smart guys. They may have some answers for us.

Nev's blue eyes raked over me for a moment before he nodded. "Fine. I can agree to that. Party at my place."

"No party," Eric grumbled.

"Glad you're bringing him," Marcus said with a laugh. "He sounds like he'll be loads of fun."

"Eat shit, Ambrose," Eric said.

"We'll see you tomorrow. Midnight," I said, wanting to get away before they argued and the plans fell through. I should have been staying away from them like I'd said I would, but what I needed to ask them wasn't something that could wait too much longer.

"It's a date," Nev said, flashing his fangs.

I swallowed, some strange emotion rushing through me as Raiden's face flashed in my head. Blood. Him, biting me as he pushed into my heat, the pain and pleasure making me weak with want. I shook my head and looked over to Eric as Nev and Marcus walked past us, engaged in their own conversation as they walked away.

"It's nothing," Eric said, confirming what I already knew.

He'd seen inside my head too.

EVERLY

"How do you know it's nothing?" I pressed.

"Because I do." This wasn't the Eric I knew. The Eric I knew would be forthcoming with me and not uptight. This Eric didn't want to talk about.

I sped up my walking and got in front of him and faced him. He let out a sigh and stopped in his tracks.

"You know something. Tell me."

"Ever, come on," he said. "I don't know anything—"

"Just like you didn't know who Shadow was?" I countered.

A frown marred his lips. "That's not fair. You know why I couldn't say anything."

"You saw the vision I saw. Both of them, didn't you? The one when I hit my head and the one that flashed in my head just now."

His gaze darted around before it finally landed on me. "Yeah."

"And you know what Raiden is really doing."

"Not really," he said. "I just know he needed to leave. I don't know the details of where he is or exactly what he's doing."

"Eric."

"Ever, come on. You want to know what I know? I know nothing. I have a shit ton of questions, not answers. It's not my place to tell you what he did, OK? I made the arrangements to make this easier while he figured his shit out. That's it. I'm sure he'll get things sorted. I can't offer anything else than that for an answer."

I studied him for a moment. I knew he wasn't telling me everything, but one very real thing kept prodding at my brain.

"I didn't fall, did I?"

He looked away from me for a moment and drew in a deep breath. "No."

"You know what really happened."

He nodded wordlessly, not meeting my gaze.

"Raiden left because of it."

He finally focused on me. "Ever, it's a bit more complicated than that. He didn't leave because of what you saw, as far as I know. He left because of what he did to you."

"What he did?"

"Yeah. It wasn't good. It's not my place to say, so you'll just have to talk to him about it, OK? He's the one with answers. I'm just the guy with questions because I know just about what you know. That's it."

I knew my line of questioning was over. He'd told me what he could, and for that I needed to be grateful. And wait. Because that's all I could do.

"WE AREN'T GOING to stay long," Eric said as we walked to Nev's place the following night. We still had no word from Raiden. Eric had gone to the Order to handle business in his place. From what I'd gathered, it hadn't gone well because Eric came back upset over whatever happened.

"OK, but this is important to me," I said as we stopped outside Nev's door.

"Ever, we both know you aren't allowed to associate outside Conexus. And we both damn well know more that it should never be Blackburn and Ambrose. Especially Blackburn, all things considering."

"I didn't have sex with him," I said, the question still lingering in my voice. I'd had time to mull it over. It didn't make sense to me, but my head felt clearer. The question did remain, though. "I think. Raiden believes it didn't happen, so I believe it didn't happen."

Eric rubbed his eyes. "Let's just get this over with. Blackburn is a cunning little asshole. He has a reason for everything he does. I'm sure we'll figure out whatever the hell his plans are soon enough. For now, I'm calling this Conexus business, so we don't get screwed if anyone finds out."

"Fair enough." I knocked on Nev's door. He answered immediately, a smile on his face.

"I was wondering when you'd get here. You're late. I didn't think Conexus ever showed up late." He held the door open and gestured for us to enter.

"You aren't exactly important," Eric grumbled, stepping inside.

Instead of getting upset at Eric's words, Nev only smiled and nodded for us to take a seat on his couch. Marcus was already perched in one of the overstuffed chairs.

I sank onto the leather with Eric beside me and watched as Nev grabbed some sodas from his fridge before placing them on the coffee table in front of us. Eric snagged a soda and cracked it open and drank.

"So. Two Conexus members in my place and they aren't kicking my ass," Nev said, settling into his seat across from us. "I honestly don't know what to say."

"You can say what you wanted to say last night. I mean, that's the reason we're here." Eric cut him a pointed look.

"Snarky, aren't you, Craft? If I recall, you were supposed to wait nearby, not on my couch."

"You opened the door and let me in. That's on you."

"Stop," I cut in. "Nev, do you need Eric to leave?"

Nev pursed his lips and tilted his head as he took Eric in. Instead of answering me, he addressed Eric. "Craft."

"Blackburn."

"I have a question for you. Your answer will depend on whether I let you party hard with us tonight."

Eric chuckled and shook his head. "Whatever, man. Ask your question."

"It's actually more than one. Still want to play?"

"Let's do it." Eric sat forward and gestured for Nev to talk.

"He's much more reasonable than Hawthorne, don't you think?" Nev looked to Marcus, who nodded.

"Anyway, question one. Are you in love with Ever?"

Eric blinked rapidly as I froze in my seat. Heat flooded my cheeks at Nev's ridiculous question.

"What?"

"I asked if you are in love with Ever. Or if you ever were."

Eric's Adam's apple bobbed in his throat for a moment before he answered. "There was a time where I felt deeply for her. She is one of my greatest and best friends."

"But love her?" Nev pressed. Marcus sat forward, watching Eric. I had no idea why this was even important to Nev, and I almost said as much when Eric spoke.

"Yes."

I stared wide-eyed at his admittance.

He cleared his throat before continuing. "I wanted her. I love her. She's my friend. In the beginning, I contemplated going for it, but I knew who she really belonged to. I backed off because I'm not the one she's meant to be with. Wasting her time like that would have hurt us both." He turned to me and gave me his gentle smile. "I do love you, Ever. But it's friendship now. You're Raiden's girl. I could never come between you two."

"Nice answer," Nev said. "Ever?"

I snapped my attention to him.

"Did you ever love Eric?"

"Why are we doing this?" I demanded. "What's the point in it?"

"Don't get touchy." Nev shrugged. "I'm just trying to get some feelers here on how to proceed. Answer the question or he leaves."

"You're an asshole," I muttered. "Yeah. I loved Eric. I still love Eric, but it's in the same way he loves me. We're friends. He was my first friend here. He saved me."

"You saved me," he said, the corner of his lips quirked into a sweet smile.

I smiled back. "We're more than even."

"Aw, how touching. OK. Next question." Nev rolled his eyes. "Craft. We all know Ever is the Mancer. We know Raiden is Shadow, and he's the Reever. That being said, if Ever were to leave Conexus to pursue. . .other opportunities, would you follow her?"

"She can't leave Conexus unless she dies," Eric said.

"OK, then say she goes rogue because she believes she's saving the world. To save it, she has to leave and join with those you deem your enemy. Do you follow her or become her enemy? Keep in mind, you claim to love her. At least in a friendship sort of way."

Eric frowned at the question and was quiet for so long I thought he wouldn't answer. "I will go where she goes."

"You'd die for her?" Marcus asked.

"Yes. Without a doubt."

"Would you, say, join a secret society on a whim for her? Without any more information other than she's going to save the world?" Nev pressed.

Eric hesitated for a moment as his gaze raked over me. "Yes."

My heart jumped into my chest at his words. I knew Eric. When Eric said something, he meant it. For him to say this was huge. I let out a shaky breath. Maybe if Eric joined, he'd be able to convince Raiden. Maybe even Damien and rest of Conexus. Eric was respected and loved among Conexus.

"OK. My final question."

Eric focused back on Nev.

"Will you join tonight?"

"Are you propositioning me, Blackburn?"

"I think I'm enticing you," Nev answered. "Will you join her? Us? Right here. Right now. Swear an oath. Become part of our inner circle. I'm opening our door to you, a Conexus member, and inviting you in. Do you accept?"

A muscle thrummed along Eric's jaw. I held my breath, wondering what he'd say and knowing it would hurt if he said no, but I could also understand why he would. What Nev was offering seemed like madness. All Eric knew was Nev was Cipher. He didn't know about Dyre. He didn't know about my grandparents or how we were trying to save the world, not doom it. His information had been wrong for so long that I understood why he'd decline. But damn, I really hoped he'd say yes.

"I accept."

The room grew so silent you could have heard a pin drop.

"Induct me. I'm in," Eric broke the silence with firm words. "I'm in wherever Ever goes."

"Strange you should agree," Nev murmured, looking as shocked as I felt. "Your General declined my invitation."

"Raiden is a logical thinker. He needs more information than I do. He has a lot at stake. He's going to be a king. If he messes up, it could weigh heavily on him. If I mess up, I'll die and be a disgrace to my family I hardly speak to. I feel confident our reasons are solid and reflect who we are as Specials. I said I'm in. Now induct me."

"Eric," I started, but he gave my hand a squeeze.

"I'm in," he repeated. "I said I'd follow you. I'm living up to it. I'm sure Raiden will too once he gets the answers he needs. I trust you, Ever."

"Thank you," I whispered, tears stinging my eyes. I wiped at them quickly as Eric turned back to Nev.

"We doing this or are you all talk?"

"I have to feed from you and Marcus will place a spell on you. If you talk about what we're doing, the curse will take hold and you'll kill who you tried to tell and yourself. It's a steep price to pay for saving the world. You will be a recruit for the time being. Once you've proven yourself, I'll let you in on some of our secrets. For now, you'll be my tool I use when I need some help."

"OK," Eric said simply, not even getting upset that Nev would be in charge. Even referring to Eric as his tool had no effect on him.

Nev and Marcus exchanged looks before they got to their feet and approached. Clearly, they were confused about Eric's response. Nev sat on Eric's left as Marcus stood over them.

"Let me be in control," Nev said.

"Do what you have to do," Eric replied tightly as Nev leaned into him.

I watched as Nev breathed him in. Eric tightened his hands into fists on his lap as Nev's lips slid up his neck. I'd never seen Nev bite anyone but me before, and it wasn't exactly like I could look down on it. But seeing it from the angle I was, I could see what an intimate thing it was.

Nev's hand traveled to Eric's face, where he cradled it for a moment before he ran his fingers through his hair. He gave his head a tug to the side. My breath caught as Nev pressed his lips to Eric's neck. Eric stilled, waiting for the bite, his chest heaving, his fists tight.

Nev's teeth sank deep into Eric's flesh, making him sag against Nev. Nev wasted no time burying his fangs deeper and drinking, the sound the Eric's blood rushing into Nev's mouth meeting my ears.

Marcus wove his spell together, saying the old words I didn't speak. A thick layer of purple magic blanketed Nev and Eric as Nev continued to feed.

Eric's hand moved to Nev's thigh, and he twisted his fingers into Nev's black pants, his breathing coming in soft gasps that sounded so sinful I thought maybe I should leave the room.

"Nevron, enough," Marcus called out as the purple spell absorbed into Nev and Eric. Eric's hand moved higher on Nev's leg as his body trembled.

Nev withdrew his fangs with a soft groan as Eric slumped back in his seat, his chest heaving.

I said a silent prayer that Nev hadn't lusted Eric. That would be too awkward for Eric. Knowing Nev the way I did, I was sure he'd make sure Eric never forgot it either.

Nev leaned into Eric again and licked the wound on his neck, sealing it shut and stopping the bleeding.

"Did it feel good?" Nev asked in a husky voice, his blue eyes skirting quickly over Eric who laid against the back of the couch, his lips parted.

Eric nodded wordlessly, still breathing hard and fast.

"D-Did you lust him?" I asked, frowning at Eric, who closed his eyes.

"No," Nev answered, wiping at his lips. "I was trying something."

"And what was that?" Marcus mused, glancing at Eric, who still had his eyes closed.

"Just to see if I could make him feel good like I do with Ever. I didn't know if it pertained only to women or just Mancers. Figured since I had a willing participant, I'd give it a go."

"It worked," Eric mumbled. "Felt so damn good."

Nev grinned, looking like the cat who got the cream.

"What was the point in it?" I demanded, watching Eric as he let out a soft, contented sigh.

"Well, for one, Eric is a pretty little thing. I've always wondered what he tasted like. *Felt* like. You should hear how many Specials would kill for a chance with him. And two, I wanted to reward him because he joined. Showing him pain seemed wrong since he so blindly believes in you. So I figured I'd see if I could make him feel as good as I made you feel. I probably didn't even come close, but it was definitely good for both of us."

I sighed and reached for Eric's hand. He twined his fingers with mine immediately.

"I-Is that all? Am I in?" he asked weakly.

"That's all. You're in. Welcome to Dyre, Eric. Now, I have a job for you." Nev's lips twisted up into that wicked smile I knew so well.

Worry crept through me. Nev never didn't things half-assed. I knew this would be no exception.

EVERLY

I blamed it on blood loss, but Eric dozed off on Nev's couch, his breathing deep and even. Nev stared at him with a tiny smirk on his lips.

"Was all that really necessary?" I asked, staring at Nev.

He shrugged. "No, but like I said, I've been dying for a taste of him." He paused. "I should have lusted him and seen where it went. Imagine having that hanging over his head." He chuckled and patted Eric's thigh before turning his attention to me.

I shook my head at him. "I agreed to meet with you tonight to talk to you about some things. I actually need help with something."

"Ah, funny you should require help because I also require it," he said. "Marcus found out some things."

I looked to Marcus, who sat forward. "I've been doing some digging. I've found out a few things about your dear Reever."

It was my turn to sit forward. "What did you find out?"

"That's he's missing and not on an Order excursion. He was spotted in London two nights ago by one of ours, who was doing some skulking around." Marcus pushed a black and white photo at me of Raiden coming out of a building, dressed all in black. I stared down at the photograph, noting the sad expression on his face.

"As much as I wish it were a strip club, he was actually coming out of one of our world's archive centers. This one isn't nearly as large as the one in Xanan, but it does house lots of information. You have to have Order clearance to even enter the building. Our man spotted him coming out and was able to get inside and take a peek at what your dear Reever was up to." Nev smiled at me.

"What was that?" I held my breath, waiting for the answer.

"He was looking up his family history on vampires. Strange, isn't it?" Nev sat back and smiled over at a passed out Eric. "I really should have lusted him."

"Nev, focus," I called out. "Why was he looking up vampires?"

"That's what we'd like to know," Marcus said. "It makes little sense. Everyone knows Raiden's mother was a psy fae and his father is a shifter. We thought maybe you'd have the answer. Because this is big, Ever. Why is the general wondering if he has vampire lineage?"

I shook my head. "I honestly don't know. He's never mentioned it to me that I can recall." I frowned, the image of him biting me on display in my head.

"What is it?" Nev pressed.

"I-I had this image. This vision of him biting me. Of Raiden feeding off me. Eric can sometimes see my visions too. He saw this one and told me it was nothing. I had this vision right before Raiden left. I don't remember it. I woke up, and he was gone and my memory was blanked out. Eric said I'd fallen. I-I know it's a lie though."

"May I look?" Nev asked softly.

"Y-You want to get inside my head?" The thought made me tense and slide further from him.

"I swear to you I won't cause you any harm. I can look in and see if there's something buried. I promise it'll be the only thing I look at." He looked so sincere that I found myself nodding.

I watched as he got to his feet and sat across from me on the coffee table. He placed his hands on my face and smiled.

"Relax," he murmured before closing his eyes.

There was a tremendous pressure in my head that made me cry out. As fast as it happened, it subsided. I could feel Nev inside my head. Each shuffle through my memories made me wince at the dull ache of his intrusion. My memories flashed before my eyes quickly as he shuffled through them, tossing them aside until I felt him pause.

Darkness passed over my thoughts. A big, black wall. Nev continued to rifle through these black thoughts, his hands trembling on my face.

He pulled away suddenly, his eyes wide and sweat dotting his forehead.

"Holy. Shit."

"What?" I reached for him, feeling like I was going to vomit. "T-Tell me."

He shook his head and looked to Eric. When he finally spoke, his voice was soft and shaky. "You said you wanted to talk to me tonight. I urge you to do it quickly."

"Nev, what did you see?" I demanded, the nausea twisting like a snake in my guts.

"I don't know what I saw. It doesn't make sense to me. I-just ask me what you needed to ask me."

My bottom lip wobbled. I still didn't have any answers. Eric was right. I only got more questions.

Damnit.

"I-I wanted to know if you knew Raiden had a brother. A twin," I whispered. "He died in childbirth. King Wesley told him the twin was born five minutes after him and he never saw him. Raiden's mother took his body to be put in her family crypt. We went there. There was no body, just an empty tomb."

Marcus and Nev exchanged looks.

"Hawthorne has a twin?" Nev asked softly, his voice shaking still.

I nodded. "That's what the king said. I had a prediction that the other was going to save me when Raiden couldn't. His brother. How is any of it possible?"

Nev paled. "I-I think you should get Eric and go."

"What? That's not how this works. You've done nothing but leave me with more questions tonight!" I protested. "I need to know what you know, Nev."

I got to my feet and glared at him. "You swore I was part of this. You promised you'd not keep secrets from me too. How can I fight a war when everything is a damn secret!"

Nev launched himself to his feet and was in my face in moments. "Many things came to light tonight, Ever. I don't have answers for you because they are still really messed up questions in my head. I'm asking you to leave so that I may sort through them. I need you to go. Please," his voice wobbled. "I'm begging you. I need to be alone right now. I promise when I get the answers you'll be who I come to. Right now. . . I just. . . can't." He stepped away from me and went to his bedroom and closed the door softly.

I stared at Marcus in confusion and shock.

"I don't know what's happening," Marcus said calmly. "But if it has him this worked up, he's going to need some time to work through it, OK? Nev doesn't back out of a promise, Ever. He'll reach out to you when he has his head sorted. In the meantime, let me help you get Craft back, OK?"

I nodded tightly and helped Marcus heft Eric to his feet. Eric groaned and his eyelids fluttered. This would not be fun hauling him all the way to the Conexus house.

"It'll be easy," Marcus said, as if reading my mind. "I'll cast him weightless. It'll be like carrying a bag of air."

Marcus said a quick spell as I stared at Nev's closed door, wondering what the hell was going on but also knowing I wasn't going to get any answers tonight.

Marcus hauled Eric over his shoulder, and I followed him out. He cast around us so we weren't seen, but it didn't matter to me.

I had been seen. Nev made sure of it. And he'd tucked it all away safely inside him, forcing me to wait.

But I had no choice.

I'd wait. I had a feeling the answer he'd give me would change everything.

RAIDEN

I'd been gone for nearly two weeks. The burning ache had long since subsided to the point where I could form coherent thoughts again. Everything I'd looked into scared the shit out of me.

None of what I learned made much sense to me, though. Vampires were born typically, not made. Many who were made didn't live past being a fledgling because the venom eventually ate through their bodies, especially if the body were a Nattie. Specials had a much higher survival rate if the blood exchange occurred.

When baby vampires were born, they were given the blood of their parents. It would solidify who they were. Without the blood, they'd turn carnal and most would likely die in the first few months of life because they required the blood of a vampire to make their lives stick. I wasn't born to vampire parents. My father is a shifter. My mother was a psy fae. I had no history on either side of my family that I could find that said I had any vampire blood within me.

So it made little sense why I was craving blood so much. And not just any blood. Ever's blood.

I was out of answers. Nothing could pinpoint what was happening to me. It had to just be my connection to Ever from our soul bond.

Maybe since I could do most abilities Specials did, this was me taking on vampirism. I didn't want the gift—or curse—but it looked like I'd gotten a healthy serving of it. I didn't even have fangs, so that made it that much more interesting.

I shifted the large parcel beneath my arm as I entered Conexus house. It was late—or early, depending on perspective — and I knew most of the members were sleeping or on patrols. Quietly, I made my way upstairs to Ever's room. I melded inside and placed the box on her desk and frowned as I took her in.

Eric laid beside her, both of them sleeping soundly. They'd fallen asleep facing one another, like maybe they'd been talking. I ground my teeth as my jealousy reared its ugly head. I knew they'd slept in the same bed together before. They'd done it over Christmas when Ever's house came under attack and I'd ordered Eric to stay with her while Damien and I took care of everything.

I shoved away my angry, jealous feelings. I trusted them both. Eric would never. And Ever. No.

I told myself I'd keep my distance and ease my way back to being close to her. All I wanted to do was kiss her and hold her and tell her how much I missed her. I didn't completely trust myself just yet, though with the strange thirst and heaven forbid someone besides Eric found out about it.

My shame and guilt were eating at me over what I'd done to my girl. It sickened me. I backed away from Ever in her bed and melded back to my room. I'd see her in the morning. I just hoped I didn't screw it up.

I AWOKE EARLY despite my late night and got up and showered. I'd spent my time away in one of my houses in the Rocky Mountains in the beginning. The fresh air helped me a great deal, or at least I felt like it did. I vowed I'd take Ever to my place in the mountains some-day. It was really beautiful, and I thought she'd love to see the view. After getting my head together, I really dug into trying to figure out what was happening. That led me to the archives in London. And more of all the damn dead ends.

After my shower, I went downstairs to see Damien puttering around in the kitchen.

"Morning," I said, opening the fridge.

"Hey, man. When did you get in?"

I pulled out a bottle of orange juice and poured a glass. "Late last night."

"Everything OK?"

I offered him a tight smile. "Best as it can be. I think I have things sorted."

"Is this one of your secrets? Because those never end well." He frowned at me, pausing the buttering of his toast.

"Like I said, I think I have things sorted."

"Good. Need a report?" He plowed on. Damien was never one to linger long on a subject. Eric was the one who preferred to talk things over until everyone was blue in the face.

"Yes."

"Nothing happened. Ever was safe. She did patrols with Eric. He didn't leave her side. In fact, they've been inseparable for the last week." He paused and licked his lips.

"What?" My heart jumped into my throat.

"It's weird. They've been doing all the night patrols together. You know no one wants to do that shit. But Eric has been putting everyone off so him and Ever can do it. I mean, it's cool for everyone else because no one wants to walk around the grounds all night. Shit sucks. But yeah. I asked him why he was doing it and he said Ever wanted more practice. I think it's more than that, but I don't know."

I nodded, hating the seed of doubt that was sprouting in my mind. Damien was right. No one liked to do patrols. I knew Eric, though. Hell, I knew Ever. Something was up they weren't telling anyone about. It wasn't an affair. It was something else.

"They're sleeping together." The words slip out of my mouth before I could stop them.

Damien widened his eyes and dropped his toast on the counter.

"Not like that," I added hastily. "Right now. They're in Ever's bed. I went in there this morning to check on her and he was in there with her."

"You don't think—"

"No," I cut him off. "Absolutely not. Eric isn't like that. Ever is faithful to me. I think it's something else. I'll talk to them and see what they say."

"OK. You're the boss. Anyway, Amara did a shit ton of bitching. Eric made her do morning patrols. She was pretty pissed off about that. The carrion nest we went to went well. Killed everything that crawled in that place. Other than that, all's well."

"Good," I said, nodding. I downed my glass of juice. "I need to see Brighton this morning." I rinsed my glass and put it in the strainer. "I'll see you later. Let everyone know we'll have a meeting at eleven."

"You got it, man." He practically inhaled his toast as I left the room. I could have easily gone back upstairs and woke Ever and hauled her into my arms, but I wanted to maintain my distance and work slowly back into getting close to her. I was terrified I'd snap like that again. Truth be told, I was worried maybe Eric told her what I'd done and what he'd had to do to make her forget it. The idea she could very well be pissed at me weighed heavily on my mind.

I doubted Eric would do that to me, but there was always a possibility.

"GENERAL, I WASN'T EXPECTING YOU," Brighton greeted me as I stepped into his office.

"My apologies, headmaster. I needed to speak with you and thought it shouldn't wait."

He gestured for me to have a seat. The moment I was in my chair, Ceres came to me and whimpered, her paw on my leg. I gave her head a pat. She licked my hand and moved back to her bed by the fireplace.

"What brings you in, General?"

"I was wondering if maybe you could help me with something." I paused for a moment and gathered myself. "Have you ever heard of a Special who wasn't a vampire getting vampire urges?"

Brighton frowned. His gaze jumped to Ceres, who perked up on her bed.

"Why do you ask?"

"I-I think perhaps I've encountered an issue. You are the only person I can think to come to and ask." I blew out a breath. "Recently, I've developed some unsavory urges to. . . feed."

Brighton's eyebrows raised high. "That's. . . odd."

"I haven't been bitten. I have no family history of vampirism. The only thing I can think is that it's my soul bond to Everly. Perhaps since I possess other abilities and this is one I lack, maybe it's coming to head." I hoped it didn't sound as ridiculous as I thought it did.

"I see." Brighton settled back in his seat and was wordless.

"Headmaster—"

"You're . . . nineteen now?"

"I am."

He nodded, deep in thought.

"There's more. I found out I have a brother. Or had a brother. Kazimir. He was born five minutes after me. He passed at birth. My mother had him buried in Ravenvale Grove, her hometown. I went there. I went to his tomb. His body wasn't there. There was a note. It said to follow the red."

Brighton got to his feet, and I watched as he went to a book on one of his shelves and pulled it out. He flipped to a page near the middle and came back and slid the book across the table from me.

I stared down at the words on the page.

Delayed Vampirism: A Spell to Keep Vampire Babies From Ascending to Their Birthright.

"What's this?"

"That, General, is an article about how there is a spell to stop vampirism in vampire infants. Rather than the baby be transformed— or ascend as vampires call it—the baby is put under a heavy magical spell that delays their carnal urges that would let them die without blood from another vampire. As you know, infant vampires die if they don't get blood from another vampire. The tradition is the father of the baby gives the blood so that he may ascend through his father's gift since the mother already gave the gift of life."

My throat tightened as I stared down at the spell. "This is complicated. How can one conjure such a spell? I've never seen magic quite so complex before."

"Indeed. A powerful Lock would be needed. However, I think it's more likely many Locks would come together for something so powerful. Perhaps three. Maybe more."

"What aren't you saying?"

"I'm saying I've never heard of a vampire being held back and delayed in his ascension. I'm saying I don't know if that's the case with you, but it's the only one I can think of. I'm saying that I don't know the answer to the question you ask. And finally, I'm saying that if you have these urges, it's of great importance that you train yourself to not attack anyone."

"Of course," I murmured.

"Have you fed?" Brighton asked softly.

"From another vampire? No," I said thickly. "But I did slip and feed off my Mancer."

"Is that why you've been absent the past few days?"

"It is. I wanted to try to find the answers. I wanted to try to strengthen my mind so that I may control the urge better. I came back because I couldn't find the answers anywhere. I can't ask my father or anyone, really." I paused and licked my lips. "I'm worried I'm not who I've always thought I was. Could I be. . . a vampire?"

Brighton let out a sigh and looked at Ceres again. "He needs to know," he murmured, as if speaking to the hellhound. Ceres let out a growl at Brighton, who grimaced and looked back to me.

"Your father is a shifter. Your mother was a psy. I don't know much past that. This is an answer you'll have to find on your own. I do urge you to keep digging."

"Thank you." I got to my feet, frustrated beyond belief. He knew something. I knew he did, but I knew Brighton well enough to know when he was digging his heels in. He wasn't going to say shit to me about it.

"Am I a vampire?" I asked, as I stopped at the door and looked back at him.

"No," he said. "You're not."

"Will I be?"

"I suppose you decide, don't you, General?"

I suppose I would decide. My answer would be no. It would always be no when it came to anything to do with vampires. They killed my mother. They took my childhood from me.

"General?" Brighton called out to me as I stepped out his door.

I looked back at him.

"Perhaps vampires are the red you should follow."

I said nothing at his words and closed the door behind me, knowing Brighton and I would have our time one day and maybe when that day came, he'd be honest with me. I prayed it came soon because shit was about to get real bad.

EVERLY

"Did Raiden come home?" I asked as I met Damien in the living room that morning.

"Yeah," he said around a mouthful of bread.

"So he's here?"

"He was here. He stepped out to go meet with Brighton."

My stomach fell. He'd returned and hadn't come to me. That was unlike him.

Or maybe he came and found me and Eric sleeping in the same bed. We'd fallen asleep talking about Dyre last night. Nev had Eric feeding him information on the Order. I knew Eric wasn't exactly giving all the info up on some things like the inner workings, but I knew when Nev asked him what happen to the dead when they were captured in the vorbex boxes he wasn't lying. He really didn't know. Raiden didn't either.

We'd fallen asleep talking about Eric's discontent with the entire Dyre business and saying he would follow because he trust me, but I knew deep down he suspected Nev was up to something. Nev was just that way. He gave off the vibe he was always up to something.

When I'd asked Nev again about what he saw in my head, he clammed up and told me he was still working out details. Figured.

"Did he say anything?" I asked.

"Like. . .that he went into your room and saw you and Eric cozied up together in your bed?" Damien lifted his brows, a tiny smirk on his lips. "No. He didn't say anything at all."

"Don't be a jerk. I need to talk to him." I reached out with my mind and frowned. He had a block up. *He was blocking me?* My heart sank.

"He's in a meeting, Ever," Damien said, as if he were reading my mind. "He's not upset with you. He's just a busy guy. I'm sure he'll sweep you up into those big arms of his the moment he walks through the door."

I looked to the door, hoping to see him walk through it. When he didn't, I wandered back upstairs and sank onto my bed. Eric left to get ready for the day. I was just about to get back up and go downstairs when a package on my dresser caught my eye. I got to my feet and went to it and brought it back to the bed and lifted the lid off.

Inside was the most beautiful gown I'd ever seen. Black lace. Blood red silk.

I pulled it out, and the skirt fell around in waves of red splendor. It was a gown fit for a princess.

"Wow," I murmured, taking it in.

A piece of paper fluttered out and fell to the floor. I swooped down and picked it up and unfolded it.

My Dearest Everly

I knew you were worried about having a gown to wear to the ball. I saw this and thought you'd look beautiful in it. I eagerly await seeing you in it, baby.

Your Reever

Shadow

I smiled and clutched the note to my chest before I took the dress to my closet and hung it.

"Meeting in fifteen minutes. Everyone get here. Our esteemed General has returned," Damien's voice rang out in my head. "And can someone bring something from the sweet shop? We're out of bread, and I want muffins."

His voice disappeared, and I rushed to my bathroom, where I

quickly fluffed my hair and dabbed on lip gloss before I smoothed down my black uniform and made my way downstairs. Everyone else had already gathered. Raiden sat in his chair, his back to me. Slowly, I walked around him and took a spot on the couch next to Eric.

"First order of business," he started without glancing in my direction. He looked tired but beautiful in his all black, his eyes dull. "We have the ball tomorrow night. That means everyone in their best attire. We will leave the Dementon grounds together and take the portal to Xanan. I need not remind you all how important it is that we all represent our region in the most professional manner. That means be respectful to the Order members and any of the dignitaries and guests." He shot a look to Damien. "And no disappearing after making an appearance."

Damien held his hands up. "I was hungry."

Raiden shook his head. "Next order of business. You guys did great taking out the carrion nest. We've been tasked with a new haunt. I received the order recently. I will head it. Everly, Eric, Damien, Mason, Brandon, and Sloane. We're the team on this. I don't expect it to be a colossal task. It seems minimal, but you all know how that goes."

Brandon let out a groan as Amanda gave him a sympathetic look.

"Third thing I want to address is the magic users need to go out on the grounds tomorrow evening before we leave and fortify our barrier. We need to make sure Dementon is protected while we're gone. I don't foresee any issues with the protection barriers already in place, but it's always good to add an extra layer."

"You got that right," Jared snorted.

"Like that time you were with that were—" Adam started.

Raiden cleared his throat. "Any questions?"

"Yeah. Where were you?" Amara demanded. I looked between her and Raiden.

He shifted in his seat. "I needed to step away."

"That's it? That's all you're going to tell us?" she pressed. "Because that's not good enough. You left your post. I want to know why."

"I had things that needed taken care of. I needed to—"

"Don't you dare say it was secret Order business because I asked my father and he said no orders were handed down. Unless you're running unsanctioned missions—"

"I am your prince," Raiden snarled, sitting forward, his aquamarine eyes flashing. "Your general. Your future king. You do not question me. Do you understand?"

She glared at him for so long that the tension became nearly unbearable.

"This meeting is over." Raiden got to his feet and went to his office without a backward glance. Everyone shifted awkwardly.

"He didn't even talk to you," Chloe said with a frown as she stared at Raiden's closed door. "What the hell?"

Amanda shot me a worried look. "Are you two fighting?"

"I-I don't think so—"

"He probably found out you and Eric were screwing while he was gone," Amara called out, looking smug. "I mean, we all know you guys spent the night together more than once. It was only a matter of time until he found out."

"Amara," Eric snapped. "Shut your mouth. You're causing problems in things that aren't your damn business."

"Do you deny it?" She crossed her arms over her chest. The entire group volleyed their gazes between Eric and Amara.

"I'm not doing this shit with you," Eric said, getting to his feet.

The door to Raiden's office opened, and he stepped out, his gaze darting over the scene. I got to my feet nervously.

"What's all the yelling?" he asked.

"Eric and Ever are screwing around behind your back. The entire time you were gone they spent it together. They did patrols together, and I know the last few nights they slept with one another," Amara shouted, pointing an accusing finger at me. "She's cheating on you, Raiden."

"Eric. Ever. My office." He turned on his heel and went into the office. Eric and I exchanged quick looks before following him, leaving our group to whisper behind us.

Once inside, we stood in front of his desk as he settled behind it.

"Sit," he commanded softly.

We did as we were told. All sorts of wild worries coursed through me as he surveyed us. He didn't look at me like he usually did. The adoration and affection weren't there. My heart clenched as I looked to my hands in my lap. He was looking at me like he used to. Before we were together. Like I was just another person for him to deal with.

"I trust nothing is going on. We can all just relax," he said. "What I do want to know is why you two are doing patrols without rotating. I assume you have a good reason for it?"

"We've been noticing a lot of activity from Blackburn and Ambrose," Eric said immediately. "We've been keeping an extra close eye on him. I heard through the grapevine he's been leaving under the cover of darkness. I was simply trying to catch him. I asked Ever to partner with me because she knows him better than anyone. I thought she'd be an asset."

Raiden nodded. "OK. I accept that. How was everything in my absence?"

If I didn't know better, I'd think Raiden was nervous as he stared at Eric. He'd still not really acknowledged me. That didn't put me at ease in the slightest.

"Damien already gave me a report," Raiden continued. "I just need yours."

"Everything was fine. Amara gave me a tough time, but nothing I couldn't handle. The carrion nest went off without a hitch. All has been quiet here," Eric said.

"Good." He pulled out a folder and shuffled through the papers. "You're dismissed."

Eric shot me a quick look as he got to his feet. I followed, not sure what to do. He said nothing and went to the door, me trailing behind him.

"I'll wait outside," Eric's voice came through my head as he left the room, closing the door firmly behind him.

I stood with my back to Raiden, knowing he was staring at me. I hadn't felt this nervous and uncertain around him since the first time we'd met, and even then I'd have lashed out at him and told him what I thought. Now I just felt lost.

"I missed you," he said softly, pulling me out of my worries.

I turned to look at him. "Did you? I didn't hear from you. You didn't come to see me when you got back. You've not even looked at me."

He got to his feet and nodded, his hands buried deep in his pants pockets. "You're right, for the most part. I'm sorry for not reaching out to you. It's just been really stressful. Don't doubt that I missed you, though. As for coming to see you, I did. You and Eric were in bed, sleeping."

"Nothing happened between us," I said immediately.

He let out a soft chuckle. "I know. I'm not really even concerned about that. I know you're my girl."

"Then what's wrong?" I asked, taking a tentative step forward. "I had a vision, and you disappeared after. What did I say? I-I don't remember it well. I don't remember much at all."

He stayed behind his desk. "The vision was just more riddles. The riddles upset me. Past that, it's me, Ever. Not you. OK? You did nothing wrong. In fact, you're perfect."

"Why are you being so distant, then?" I took another step forward. He shuffled back toward his window. "Shadow? Talk to me. No secrets, remember?"

"I can't," he whispered, his eyes wavering. "I'm still trying to figure it out. Believe me when I say it's not you. It's me. I-I think I took on a new ability and I'm trying to deal with it."

"What is it? I could help."

"The thing is, you make it worse. It's almost. . . painful to be so close to you. I thought it would stop, or I'd be able to control it, but it's not as simple as that. It's hurting me."

"What kind of ability is it?" I didn't step forward this time, worry coursing through me. I'd never seen him look so vulnerable before. So worried. So. . . afraid. He'd let the fearless mask of leader and prince fall away, leaving the worried man he was in its place.

"That's the thing. I went to Brighton this morning to talk to him about it and he doesn't know. It's just. . . dangerous." His Adam's apple bobbed in his throat. "I want to haul you into my arms and kiss you. Push everything off my desk and take you on top of it. I can't though. I don't want to hurt you. I'm supposed to protect you. I just need time to figure it out, OK? I love you so damn much. It's killing me to stay away."

"I love you too. I want to help you," I said, taking a small step forward.

He immediately backed away. "Stay away. I don't know what I'll do if you get too close."

"You won't hurt me," I said, moving closer.

He closed his eyes and breathed out. "Everly. Please. I couldn't live with myself if I screwed up again."

I closed the distance between us, noting how tense he was. I stared up at him and rested my hand on his chest. His heart hammered hard and fast beneath my fingers. My heart matched his.

"Tell me what the ability is so I can better understand it."

He squeezed his eyelids closed as I moved my hand up his chest and cradled his face. The rough stubble grazed my palm as I studied him. The torment he bore was real. It ebbed through me too, making my chest constrict and my breathing pick up.

"I'm not afraid, Shadow. I trust you."

"I don't trust me," he whispered. "Already I can feel it."

"What is it?"

"I-I want to throw you down on my desk and push myself through your heat. I want to sink my teeth into your sweet, tender flesh and devour every last drop of you there is. I want to keep you deep inside me forever."

"You want to . . . bite me?" I stared up at him in confusion.

He nodded tightly, a muscle thrumming along his jaw.

"Then do it," I whispered. "If you need it, I'm here for you."

"Everly, don't say that. I don't want to be this monster and you're spurring me on. Don't tempt a monster with acts such as these, baby. I-I almost killed you last time."

"Last time?"

"I-I fed on you. That's why I left. I bit you and drank from you. I couldn't stop. You were on the cusp of death. I brought you back. I'm so sorry. I promised to keep you safe and I hurt you," he rasped, the pain flashing deep in his eyes.

"Raiden—"

"Please," his voice shook. "I don't want anyone to know what's happening to me. I can't become whatever this is."

"Then you need to feed and learn to control it," I said gently. This was what Nev had seen in my head. He was just as confused by it as I was. Raiden hated vampires. To know he ached for blood and had taken action on it was a hard pill to swallow. I knew he was struggling with it. That broke my heart. I didn't want him to struggle. I wanted to take whatever was hurting him and keep it for myself so he'd feel better. We weren't at a place that would allow such things, so the next best thing was control. He needed to control it. Just like I needed to control my abilities.

He shook his head vehemently. "I refuse to become this . . . thing."

"You can't run from your destiny," I whispered. "Believe me. And if I'm it, you won't get far. I will keep your secret. It's not just yours to bear. It's also mine. We're a team, remember?" I hated I was almost positive Nev had seen it. That may put a kink in my promise. But it wasn't like I'd come out and told Nev. He'd had a look around in my head. Had I known it was this, I'd have not let him in.

"I remember," he murmured, staring down at me with eyes filled with so much love it made my heart jump. "I-I think it's the one ability I don't have. As your Reever, I should be able to wield them all."

"So wield them, Reever," I whispered, pushing my hair over my shoulder. "Do with me what you will."

He licked his lips, his eyes zeroed in on my pulse point on my neck.

"Maybe this is just one step closer to us getting to where we need to be," I said.

"I don't want to be a vampire," he choked out, tearing his gaze away from my neck. "I don't want people to know what sort of monster I've become. I hunt vampires. I don't want to be one."

"You aren't a monster. You're a Reever," I shot back, taking his hand in mine and kissing his palm. "My Reever. Do what you need to do. I accept all the parts of you, Raiden. I will blood oath it."

"Do you know what a blood oath does?"

I shook my head. I had no clue. I only knew Nev threw the term around a lot and it seemed like a big deal.

"It's a vow. You would become mine to feed on. I already own your soul and your body, my love. I can't take your blood."

"I'm giving it to you," I whispered. "I want you to have it."

His gaze darted to my neck again. "What if it's the last straw? What if by doing this we unlock some nightmare? Something we can't come back from? We don't know what we're doing, Ever. You know we don't."

"We're already living in a nightmare. What if by doing this we can end this war and find out who the bad guys really are? We can save so many lives. We can run away together and never look back."

"Or we rule a kingdom of ash and death," he murmured, looking pained again.

"We won't. I won't let you fall, just like you promised to not let me. I hate seeing you hurting. Take my blood. I give it freely." I went to my knees and stared up at him. "My king. My general. Please."

He let out a shaky breath as he stared down at me. His fingers brushed against my jaw. My lips. They trailed down to my neck, where he lovingly brushed his thumb along my pulse point.

"I would devour you," he said thickly.

"I'm yours to devour. I blood oath it." I pulled the dagger he'd given me and made to swipe it over my palm, but he reached out with lightening fast reflexes and tugged the blade away. It clattered to the floor.

"Blood oaths require a bite," he murmured, taking my hand and bringing me to my feet. "Each must bite the other. It's a vampire oath. I-I don't even know if it would work between us since neither of us are vampire."

"Then there's no harm in trying," I said.

"Perhaps not."

"And if you can drink from me when you need to while we figure this out, I think it would make everything easier."

"OK," his voice trembled.

I looked at him to see the turmoil on his face, but it was quickly dwindling away as a look of hunger swept over his handsome features.

I tilted my head nervously for him and swallowed down my fear and panic. I trusted Raiden. We could do this. For him, I could do this.

He squeezed his eyelids closed for a moment before he placed his hand on my hip and tugged me forward.

"Everly?" he murmured.

"Yes?"

"I'm sorry."

I didn't get a chance to respond because he leaned in and he sank his teeth deep into my neck, his grip on my hip painfully tight.

Pain. So much pain. I buckled beneath it. Then the most delicious warmth washed over me. I sagged against his hard body as he held me, his teeth embedded deep in my flesh as he drank.

So many delicious currents flowed through me. Lights popped off behind my eyelids as he clung to me, drinking deeply. I gripped his biceps as soft gasps left my lips, a heat flooding between my legs. As much as I wanted to rub my body against his, I was paralyzed to do anything but succumb to his bite.

He pulled back, his chest heaving, his lips bloody. His aquamarine eyes glowed for a moment before he swallowed.

"You have to bite me now. I-I'll weave the spell."

I stared up at him in a daze. "W-Where do I bite you?" My blood was drizzling down my neck and dampening my white button down.

He sat in his chair and brought me onto his lap and tilted his head. "Here."

I'd never in my life envisioned myself biting someone and drinking their blood. The idea wasn't one I thrived on, but this was Raiden. I'd do it for him. I wasn't completely turned off at the idea of making this bond with him.

I just didn't want to hurt him. I wasn't a vampire. Sinking my teeth deep into someone's flesh made me uneasy.

"I'll be OK," he said, his voice trembling. "Just drink."

I steadied myself and pressed my lips to his neck. He stiffened beneath me as I gathered my courage.

I opened my mouth and bit him hard. He hissed beneath the pain, his hands gripping me around the waist so hard I almost withdrew because it was hurting me.

"H-Harder," he choked out. "Deeper."

I dug deeper as a low groan left his lips, the sound of the pain he was in making me cringe.

"D-Drink," he rasped.

I sucked against his neck as his blood spurted past my lips in thick, copious amounts. He tasted sweet with a bite of iron.

"Bindarios sola faet mori e-el mortae. Crimsonia p-pura bindarios esa Everly. C-Crimsonia pura bindarios es R-Raiden. Mortae esa crimsonia. Lifea esa crimsonia. B-Bindarios."

I felt the heat of the spell engulf us as I continued to drink. He let out a soft moan that sent a flurry of butterflies straight to my core.

"More," he choked out. "P-Please. More."

I sucked harder, drawing more of his blood into my mouth and swallowing him down. His breathing picked up as the tension left his body. With my mouth still on his skin, I shifted so I was straddling him. His hands immediately gripped my ass and rocked me against his thick, hard length as he continued to moan softly.

The warmth built in my center, and I came undone against him, my vision dotting in sparkles again. He followed, gasping my name as he rocked against my aching heat. I pulled my teeth from him and watched as his wound knit itself back together.

A gasp slipped past my lips and onto his as he crashed his mouth against mine.

"Are you OK?" he asked breathlessly as we broke apart.

I nodded. "Are you OK?"

"Much better. So much better."

"And us? We're OK?"

He closed his eyes for a moment before opening them. "Always, Everly."

I buried my face in his neck, breathing in his scent and feeling closer to him than I'd ever felt before.

"Our secret," he murmured, his hold on me tightening. "Me and you. Forever."

I nodded against his chest, anxiety blossoming in my chest. "Our secret."

He pressed a fierce kiss to the top of my head and clung tighter to me, like if he let me go even for a moment he could lose me.

"I-I think I'm becoming a vampire," he choked out, so much agony in his words they made tears spring to my eyes. I'd have to figure out a way to get Nev to keep his mouth shut about this. Maybe Eric could help with that.

I could keep Raiden's secret from the rest of the world.

Our secret.

Our blood oath.

Even if it terrified me.

Even if it ended up getting me killed for good.

To Be Continued in Fatal Promises
Thank you for reading Blood Oath. Please consider leaving your review.
Join K.G. Reuss's Renegade Readers on Facebook for more updates on releases.

ABOUT THE AUTHOR

Affectionately dubbed Queen of Cliffy, Suspense, Heartbreak, and Torture by her readers, USA Today bestselling author K.G. Reuss is known mostly for making readers ugly cry with her writing. A cemetery creeper and ghost enthusiast, K.G. spends most of her time toeing the line between imagination and forced adulthood.

After a stint in college in Iowa, K.G. moved back to her home in Michigan to work in emergency medicine. She's currently raising three small ghouls and is married to a vampire overlord (not really but maybe he could be someday).

K.G. is the author of The Everlasting Chronicles series, Emissary of the Devil series, The Chronicles of Winterset series, The Middle Road (with co-author CM Lally) Black Falls High series and Seven Minutes in Heaven with a ridiculous amount of other series set to be released.

Sign up for her newsletter here:

https://tinyletter.com/authorkgreuss

Join her Facebook reader group for excerpts, teasers, and all sorts of goodies.

https://www.facebook.com/groups/streetteamkgreuss

ALSO BY K.G. REUSS

May We Rise

As We Fight

On The Edge

When We Fall

Double Dare You

Double Dare Me

Church: The Boys of Chapel Crest

Ashes: The Boys of Chapel Crest

Stitches: The Boys of Chapel Crest

Emissary of the Devil: Testimony of the Damned

Emissary of the Devil: Testimony of the Blessed

The Everlasting Chronicles: Dead Silence

The Everlasting Chronicles: Shadow Song

The Everlasting Chronicles: Grave Secrets

The Everlasting Chronicles: Soul Bound

The Chronicles of Winterset: Oracle

The Chronicles of Winterset: Tempest

Black Falls High: In Ruins

Black Falls High: In Silence

Black Falls High: In Chaos

Black Falls High: In Pieces, A Novella

Hard Pass

Kings of Bolten: Dirty Little Secrets

Kings of Bolten: Pretty Little Sins

Kings of Bolten: Deadly Little Promises

Printed in Great Britain
by Amazon